I0621162

CANDY

JUSTIN M. WOODWARD

SIMPLE BICYCLE PUBLISHING

ALSO BY JUSTIN M. WOODWARD:

The Variant

Tamer Animals

This one is for the members of Justin M. Woodward Fan Club, for cheering Candy on, and for Judy, for always believing in me.

ACKNOWLEDGMENTS

There are so many people to thank! First, I want to thank my wife Alison who hastily worked every week to edit this story as I wrote it, I love you! Thank you, Chaz Garner, for churning out some great cover art at a last minute's request. Thanks to each and every one of you who read Candy week after week and kept me going! And thank you to everyone who has ever supported any of my work. You're all badasses.

Special Thanks:

Judy Haigh, J.Z. Foster, François Vaillancourt, Melissa Lucas, Christina Arico, Katie Vaughn, Ashley Drevyanko, Beth Gahring, Dominic Lagonigro, Mary Ayers, Holly Torres, David E. Thomas, Krista Dawson, Cricket Winters, Beth Barlow, and Eric Whitney.

All around the mulberry bush,
The monkey chased the weasel,
The monkey thought t'was all in fun,
Pop! Goes the weasel.

1

HINDSIGHT

My name is Candy Tran. I'm sure you've got a pretty good mental image of me going on in your head right now. In your head I've got pink hair, I'm wearing a schoolgirl outfit, and I am 100% Asian.

Or, wait, I know: I'm a stripper, right? No. Actually, I'm about twenty pounds overweight, my skin is the color of liquid paper, and I've just got way too much eyeliner.

I'm a dumbass, okay?

I guess you're wondering what the hell I'm going on about. I'll give you some perspective. As my old pappy used to say, "Sit down and let me talk atcha!"

So, are you sitting? Okay, here goes.

I am on trial for murder. I'm recording this because I have to. I'm recording this because the story has to be told and because my life depends on it.

Oh my God, you're thinking. You're a walking cliché. And I know, I know, it seems like that's the case. Like I'm some Instagram-loving-attention-whore. Like my Twitter handle is xxQueenOfDarknessxx. No, okay?

I was a normal person before all of this. Well, my life was

fairly normal anyway. I was a Church-going, tax-paying, library-card-holding citizen.

Before all of this.

No, my life depends on this because this is the only way I can express what really happened in detail. I have to prove my innocence. I'm going to do my best to tell the story in a way that really helps you to feel like you were there. Because if you see things through my eyes, you'll understand why this story is so important. So, if you're hearing this, please hear me out. It's going to take a while.

—

MY DAD WAS ABSOLUTELY OBSESSED with that movie *Planes, Trains, and Automobiles*. You know, the one where the one guy accidentally shoves his hands into the other guy's ass in a hotel room. Does that tell you anything? Yes, I was named after John Candy, the fat guy from *Uncle Buck*. Uncle fucking Buck. I'm not shitting you. My dad's foster family is like one-quarter Vietnamese, so that's where the Tran came from. And I guess my parents just didn't see the problem in making people think I'm a Vietnamese transgender woman before they even get to know me.

But that's not why we're here. I just had to tell you so you wouldn't think less of me just because of my name. I'm sorry, it's just that you can only be called 'JonBenét Candy' so many times before you stab yourself through the brain with literally anything you can find. So, let's just not talk about my name again, okay?

Well, I guess you could say it all starts when I meet Nick.

Nick and I start dating in the 10th grade, and of course, we're soulmates. I mean who isn't ready to commit to their life partner when they're fifteen?

Nick introduces me to this podcast called *The Last Podcast on the Left*, and it fucks me up big time. I mean you don't even understand. Like, before the podcast I was attending weekly Bible groups and hanging out with youth group people. And I want to be the first to point out that I'm not blaming the podcast for what happens.

Do you remember the girl who basically told her boyfriend to kill himself and she ended up getting prison time when he finally did it? Well, I'm a believer that while she's a pretty terrible person, she's not a murderer. Nobody forced her boyfriend to do what he did. I say that because I want to express how much I don't blame anyone but us for what happens, or, at least for how it starts.

I said I was innocent, but I'm not totally innocent. I'm just innocent of 99% of the crimes and 100% of the deaths. I truly was in the wrong place, at the wrong time, for a long time.

Okay, I'll get back to the story here. Back to high-school. Walk the halls with me as I take you through my story.

So, there is this guy who used to hang around school practically every day, waiting for the bell to ring at the end of the day. His name is Ken Carothers. He had graduated about 14 years prior and his little brother Todd is my classmate. Ken is thirty-two years old, he's a registered sex-offender, and he's hanging out in the high-school parking lot, hitting on teenagers.

Well, Ken gets arrested on multiple charges halfway through our Junior year, and Todd becomes the target of a shitload of verbal abuse.

The thing is, when your creepy older brother is accused

of rape, it's hard not to hear people talking. Todd isn't dealing with the pressure very well. His older brother was accused of raping a TWELVE-year-old girl and then choking her to death. Her body was discovered in a creek about five miles from his house, and Ken's DNA was all over her. Her name was Jenny George. There was a memorial service for her in the town civic center. It was a big deal.

Todd kind of starts hating me in the middle of 5th period Social Studies. I'm passing notes—I know, I'm lame—with my friend Jordan Smith when my life changes.

Jordan and I, we're chatting—okay, gossiping—about Todd's older brother Ken and the girl named Jenny George.

Well, I'll just tell you, I fuck up big time.

Me, I'm trying to be cute and pass the note to Jordan's desk by flicking it like a little football. Problem is, I was never good at that game. I miss Jordan's desk, and that little piece of fucking paper hits our teacher in the ass.

Mrs. Parker is kind of pissed to say the least, mostly because the class won't stop laughing. So, you guessed it, she reads the note aloud in front of the entire class. This would include the part where I say that somebody ought to take Todd out before he hit the ripe old age of thirty-two. Before he ended up like Ken.

It's a joke, okay? Like, in pretty bad taste, but still. I'm joking about something that shouldn't be joked about, and I am made aware of that fact very quickly during my trip to the principal's office.

Todd isn't in that class, but I mean, it's high school. He finds out about it like immediately after it happens.

The school decides to make an example out of me and sends me to Alternative School for nine days. It's basically prison for students. You know, I'm in there with the real troublemakers. The ones who pull out each other's hair during fights and start trouble over what color shirt people wear. I suffer in silence for what feels like nine years rather than days. I don't know, I guess it doesn't matter anymore, but I swear they came down on me WAY too hard. They say it was because I had caused potentially irreversible damage to a young man's life. I think Todd is being a fucking baby. I do feel bad about it, but he knows it's true. It's not like he didn't already know what people said.

I don't actually think Todd is all that bad though. To tell the truth, I actually had a crush on him before I met Nick.

Also, before Todd's brother was on the news.

I would absolutely *never* tell Nick that though. Like, cross my heart and hope to fucking DIE. Because Nick hates Todd. It's almost like he has a sixth sense about my FORMER attraction to Todd.

Nick doesn't know that Todd started talking to me again in our Senior year either. It's strange how it happened—considering our past—but we actually started like, talking, talking. So, there's another thing to hate about me. Now I'm a cheater.

We only had sex once. It's just something that happened, as they say.

Right. I know what I did was wrong, trust me when I say I think it's probably the biggest mistake I've ever made.

Todd and I had a falling out, and he did this thing where he texted me all the time, hoping Nick would accidentally see something. Well, Nick almost DID see something one time, and it was a dick. Todd had sent me a picture of his penis with the message: "Miss this?"

I didn't.

I actually smashed my phone when I knocked it out of Nick's hand. Nick heard the text-message alert while I was in the bathroom. We were at my parents' house watching TV. I came into my room and saw Nick reaching for my phone. I could see there was a dick right there on the screen, but Nick was oblivious. I slapped the phone out of his hand and it smashed into seven million pieces.

Nick was dumbfounded; I just told him that my hand slipped. He asked if I had ever heard of Otter boxes.

When I got my new phone that weekend, the first thing I did was text Todd that I would kill him if he ever did anything like that again.

Todd left me alone after that, and I've begun to feel pretty bad about what I've done to Nick. Nick and I started out so strong, it just feels weird being committed to someone for so long at such a young age. I just can't bring myself to tell him what I've done.

Things with us get better, and we fall into a deep obsession with *The Last Podcast on the Left*. Like, it's all we ever talk about. We discuss the Dahmer crime scene photos in all their gruesome glory, we laugh at all the stupid jokes. We're swimming in our own morbid obsession.

One night, we're listening to the show, and Nick pauses his phone. "You remember Dexter?" He says.

I say, "Do you mean Michael C. Hall Dexter, or like ginger midget Dexter?"

"Michael C. Hall," he says. "The serial killer one."

"Yeah," I say. "I remember Dexter."

"Yeah," he says, "well I think somebody ought to do what Dexter did, but for real. You know, kill the evil people of the world. Like there's just so many evil people out there right now doing terrible shit to people. I just think somebody ought to kill 'em."

Me, I'm trying to figure out a Rubik's Cube. Not looking up from the cube, I say, "Well you better get on that."

Nick laughs.

—

TWO MONTHS LATER, it's time for graduation. Out into the real world and all that. The school holds a party for all the graduation seniors after the ceremony. The school gym is decorated like it was prom and they even hired a live band for us. Nick and I go to the party even though it seems pretty lame. You only graduate from high school once I guess.

We're standing by the drink table when Nick's friend, Ryan Green walks over and starts whispering something to Nick.

"Hey, what's the secret?" I ask.

Nick turns to me, and he looks like shit. All of the color has drained from him like a watercolor painting in a bathtub.

"What is it?" I ask again.

"Ken Carothers escaped from jail today," he says. "They were supposed to be shipping him up to a higher-security facility. The guards looked away for one second and Ken got one of their guns and shot them both."

"Oh shit!" I say. "Where is he now?"

Nick, his face as white as a sheet, he says, "Nobody knows."

"I don't know what you're so afraid of," I say. "He's not going to rape *you.*"

"It's not funny," Nick says. "This guy is a real sick fuck! Did you not hear the part where he shot and killed two guards?"

"Okay, okay," I say. "Let's just go home. This party is lame anyway."

We leave the stupid party, and Nick drives me home.

Later that night is when the horror begins.

—

MY PHONE DINGS, and the screen illuminates my bedroom. I reach over and grab the phone, it's 12:35 in the morning.

Nick's text reads: come outside.

I sit up in bed and rub my eyes. I slip on some shoes and make my way quietly through the house, even though my parents sleep like corpses.

Nick is waiting by his car which is parked at the curb.

"What the hell are you doing here?" I ask.

Nick smiles. He has blood on his shirt. He says, "You know how we talked about how this world needed a Dexter?"

"Nick," I say, "you're scaring me."

"Don't be scared," he says. "Just come with me."

For some reason I can't explain, I get in his car. I think maybe it's the shock. I don't know. I listen to Nick tell me how he had seen Ken Carothers walking the streets on his way home from my house.

"I followed him," he says. "He went down a dark alley and I thought to myself, 'Not today. You won't kill again.'"

In a daze, I ask what happened next.

"I parked at the end of the alley," he says. "And I followed him for a while. He was looking real suspicious, like creeping around."

"Jesus, Nick. He had a gun!" I say.

"You mean this?" Nick pops open the glove compartment and out falls a police issue Smith & Wesson. Nick giggles like a schoolgirl.

"Tell me what is going on right now!" I say. "This isn't funny!"

Nick parks the car. "I'll do more than tell you, Candy," he says. "Let me show you."

Reluctantly, I get out of the car, wishing I was wearing more than just a pair of running shorts and a ratty Misfits t-shirt.

Nick, as he's walking, he's saying that he will be seen as a god.

"It's right here," he says. "Here's the son of a bitch."

There is a body lying among trash bags and broken beer bottles. The clothes are torn and blood-soaked.

"You see?" Nick says. "Now he can't end up like Dahmer or Gacy. You know this is a good thing, Candy. We talked about this."

My voice shaking, I say, "This is murder, Nick."

Nick crosses his arms. "I thought you'd be proud," he says. "I really don't understand you."

I'm not listening to Nick. I'm looking at Ken. At his face. "Turn on your cellphone flashlight," I say.

I'm leaning way too close to the body when I see his face in the light.

I hear Nick whisper, *"Oh shit."*

The lifeless corpse in the deserted alley isn't Ken Carothers. It's the body of his little brother, Todd.

2

OH-OH HERE SHE COMES

I KNOW WHAT YOU'RE THINKING. WHY DOES NICK HAVE A police issue Smith & Wesson if it was Todd that he killed instead of Ken? Or, did you miss that part? It's okay, it took me a minute, too. Well, as I said before, this story is going to take a while.

Right now, I'm standing in a dark alley looking at a murder victim. If you can imagine, I'm not exactly ready to cope with any of this.

Nick, he says, "I swear to God I didn't know it was Todd." He says, "My God, Candy, what do I do?"

Me, I'm just staring like a nosy bitch eyeing a car accident. I can't look away. My lips try to form words, my throat makes a strange sound, but I can't seem to speak.

Nick, as he's pacing, he asks aren't I going to say something?

"Nick," I say. "What did you stab him with?"

"A fucking knife, Candy," Nick says. "What do you think?"

I ask Nick if it's the knife I gave him for Christmas he's

talking about. I ask if it's the one that has our names carved into the handle.

"Yeah," Nick says. "So what if it is?"

Looking down at the bloody mess, I ask, "Where is the knife now?"

Nick, he looks like someone who just realized the cat was in the dryer when he turned it on. He pats his pockets. He walks back to his car. "I'm sure it's in here," he says. "Somewhere."

Nick searches his car about three times over before deciding the knife isn't there.

"Nick," I say. "It's pretty fucking important that you find that knife right now." I say, "Are you sure you didn't drop it near the body?"

Understand that the only reason I'm as calm as I am, is because that knife has my name on it, and I need it found immediately.

Nick searches the body and the ground around it. And he's touching everything with his bare hands, of course. And in this moment, I just hate him so much. I don't advocate murder, ever, but Nick can't even get the basics right.

"Is it here or not?" I ask.

Nick turns and looks at me. He's freaking out. Tears are in his eyes.

"Your façade is fading," I say.

Nick asks if I think this is funny. "Because it's not," he says. "I'll go to jail for the rest of my life," he says.

Me, I'm finding it hard to believe someone can be so incredibly dense. I'm thinking of how there will be text messages on Todd's phone from me saying that I would kill him if he ever did anything like that again. I'm thinking how I can't tell Nick this piece of information. I go with what I *can* say.

"Nick," I say. "Do you not remember when I got in trouble for passing notes with Jordan?"

"Yeah," he says. "What's your point?"

"My point," I say, "is that I said in the note that somebody should kill Todd. Did you seriously forget that?"

"I guess I did," Nick says. "Fuck."

"And," I say. "The knife has our NAMES on it, Nick." We're not even getting to the real meat of the issue here. I haven't even begun to tell Nick what I think about what he's done. At this point, I'm treating him like a shock victim, because that's what he is. After I make sure I can't be connected to this, I could care less what happens to Nick. He's really fucked up this time.

"There's only one thing we can do," Nick says. "We have to get rid of the body."

I ask Nick if he came up with that one on his own.

"We have to get some trash bags. Maybe some sponges and some bleach." He says, "I can't put him in my car like this."

I ask Nick what he plans on doing with Todd after he gets him in his car.

"I don't know," Nick says. "Please just get the stuff while I think. I'll come up with something."

I say, "Why do I have to go get the stuff?"

Nick asks if I'd rather stay with the body.

—

I'M WALKING down the cleaning aisle in Walmart while Hall

& Oates sing *Oh-oh here she comes.* They sing, *watch out boy, she'll chew you up.* They warn, *She's a maneater.*

Well what the fuck?

I just start laughing like Chunk being offered a Baby Ruth. And there's this guy, his name tag says his name is Buck, he asks if I'm finding everything okay. I tell him it's surprisingly easy to find everything at three in the morning, thank you. I tell him I might have to start coming at three AM every time I come to Walmart. We both laugh.

I approach the only cashier is this miserable fucking place and I look into my cart. I've got giant trash bags, two gallons of Clorox bleach, and some rags. And, get this, I add a pack of gum. At this point, I don't even know why I bother.

The cashier, her name tag says her name is Katrina. With her right hand she's scanning my items and throwing them into a blue bag. With her left hand she's texting. I'm not sure she even realized what happened. For once, I'm completely content with the apathy of a cashier at Walmart.

Ask me if I'm handling everything okay. Well, I'm not a psychologist but I'm pretty sure I'm handling it TOO okay.

I return with Nick's car and find Nick sitting on the ground with his head in his hands. I toss him the bags. He looks through them and sighs.

"Where are the gloves?" He says.

I tell him that he didn't mention gloves.

"I thought it was obvious," Nick says. "I mean come on, Candy. That's like the first rule of getting away with a crime."

"Here's the thing about that," I say. "If you hadn't killed a person tonight, we wouldn't need gloves. Because there wouldn't be any reason for me to be touching a dead body tonight."

"I told you," Nick says. "I thought it was Ken. I saw a gun, and it just looked like him, okay? So, I thought I was doing the right thing."

Nick, he just doesn't get it, and I can't deal with that right now.

"Look," I say. "Take a fucking trash bag and stick your arms inside of it and then grab him like that." I don't even remind him that he's already touched Todd with his bare hands in several places.

Nick says, "Like when you pick up dog shit at the park?"

"Yeah," I say. "Just like that."

Nick asks if I'm helping. I'm not. You can call me a bitch if you want to. But damn, I didn't kill the guy.

I watch Nick shove Todd's body into a black industrial sized trash bag like an old teddy bear. The box on the ground, it reads: Glad.

I ask, "Do you know what you plan to do with him?"

Nick, he's clearly pissed at me for making him do this by himself. He ignores me. He's down on his hands and knees, rubbing bleach into concrete. He says, "Is this even going to get the blood out?"

I tell him I don't know.

We put the body in the backseat of Nick's car. Nick looks like a butcher.

"What do they always say on the show?" Nick says. "About hiding bodies? Where's the best place to do it?"

I ask, "Are you seriously placing your future in the hands of Henry Zebrowski?"

"First of all," Nick says, "there are two other guys involved in The Last Podcast on the Left. Secondly," he says, "they've done their research on this shit, they know what gets people caught and what doesn't."

As stupid as it sounds, he's right. "I guess," I say, "I guess the best place would probably be a grave. Nobody looks in graves."

Nick drives the car to the local cemetery. He turns off the headlights and drives the perimeter of the graveyard. "It's our lucky day," he says. Pointing, he says, "There's an empty one right over there."

There's a small excavator sitting on a plot near the back of the cemetery.

"It's probably one they're going to fill later today," he says.

He parks the car behind the excavator and I help him pull the body out of the back seat. The hole looks to be at least six feet deep and probably eight feet long. A shovel is planted into the ground like the American flag on the moon. Nick looks down into the hole.

"Go on," I say. "Jump in."

Nick stares into the hole. "How will I get out?" He says.

"Nick," I say. "I thought you were going to be seen as a god?"

He sits down and lets his feet dangle into the grave. He sighs and jumps in. I toss the shovel down into the hole.

"You'll just have to dig enough to cover him up with," I say.

Nick starts digging. I ask him if he wants me to play some Slayer. Make him feel more badass.

Nick digs a body-sized cavity in the bottom of the grave. "Alright," he says. "Toss him in."

I walk to the car and grab another trash bag from the box. Sticking my arms into the plastic, I'm wondering if I've made good life choices.

"Candy?" Nick says. "Are you still there?"

I tell him to stop being a bitch.

"How about *you* stop being a bitch?" Nick says. "I'm not having a good time here, okay?" He says, "I know I fucked up. I'm sorry, Candy. I don't know why I did what I did."

I walk over to Todd's body and grab one of his feet through the two trash bags. Luckily for me, Todd wasn't a big guy. It's fairly easy to get him into the hole. The body makes a sick slamming sound into the fresh earth. Nick wipes sweat from his forehead using the back of his arm. Using his foot, he positions the body in the hole. He starts to shovel earth over Todd's body.

"Nick," I say. "Your clothes are covered in Todd's blood. You need to ditch them."

"I can get rid of them later," Nick says. "I'm not stripping right now."

"You need to bury them with the body," I say. "You can't have someone finding them. You'd be fucked."

Nick, he's still shoveling earth. He says, "But if my clothes are found here, I'd be tied to it just the same."

"Nick," I say. "I don't know if you've thought about this, but if anyone finds *anything* down here we're shit out of luck." I say, "That's kind of the whole point. This is the safest place to hide something. Tomorrow, Todd will have an upstairs neighbor."

Nick knows I'm right. He just doesn't want to strip out here in the middle of the night.

There's a lot of things I don't want to do.

Nick strips to his underwear, tosses his bloody clothes in with Todd, and begins to cover the body. Once we're both satisfied that the body can't be seen, Nick throws the shovel out of the hole and climbs up.

—

TWO DAYS GO by and I can't stop thinking about the missing knife. After Nick dropped me off at my house on the night of the murder, we haven't spoken. I see a piece on the news about how the little brother of the recently escaped rapist was missing. Immediately after the story was done airing, my phone rings.

Nick says, "I think we're good. They don't have a clue." He asks if we can meet. I hang up the phone.

I'm sitting at the dinner table pretending to read a book about a guy who grows horns out of his head in the middle of the night. I can't concentrate.

That damn knife. We're not *good.*

My dad walks into the kitchen and plops the mail down on the table. He says we need to talk about college, even if it's just the community one.

"Absolutely," I say, still looking at the book. Dad, he's sifting through bills and collection threats when he says, "Hey Candy Trandy, you've got mail." He hands me a yellowed envelope. On the front, written with marker, is my first name, followed by my address. There is no return address.

My dad looks down at the book I'm holding. "Joe Hill," he says. "Sounds like a fake name." And he leaves the room.

I check to make sure I'm truly alone. My hands shake as I open the envelope. Photographs spill out. There is also a note. The pictures are face down on the table, and I really don't want to turn them over. I build up the courage and flip them. There are pictures of me and Nick standing over Todd's body. There are shots of us putting him in the grave. There are multiple angles of each. I look at the small slip of paper included in the envelope. There's an address on one side: **435 Edgewood Ln.**

I flip the paper over slowly and my heart sinks when I read the message: It's a lovely knife.

3

DOGHOUSE

I'M SITTING AT THE TABLE AND I FEEL LIKE ONE OF THOSE people at the end of that movie *Donnie Darko*. The camera pans around me, and Gary Jules sings *It's a very, very, mad world.*

I feel like I'm going to be sick. My dad walks back into the room, and he says, "Hey Candy, didn't you know that kid that went missing?" He says, "What was his name?"

Trying to hide the contents of the envelope, I tell him, "His name is Todd." I ask, "What makes you think I know him?"

"Well, don't you?" he asks.

"I did," I say.

"Well," my dad says, "I wouldn't say *did*, just yet. They might find him." He walks back out of the room.

I'm thinking that I really hope they *don't* find him. I'm thinking that would be it for me. There is no explaining this now.

Right now, I'm clutching the envelope with the evidence. As much as I don't want to, I pick up my phone and find Nick's name. I press send.

Nick says, "Hey. You have a change of heart?"

"Nick," I say, "I think we do need to meet."

Nick asks if he can come over now. I tell him I don't think it's the best idea. I don't know who is watching the house.

"No," I say. "We need to meet somewhere else."

"Okay," Nick says. "I know where we can meet. Let's pay our respects." He hangs up the phone. I'm starting to wonder if we'll ever say "goodbye" again.

—

NICK IS the only other person at the cemetery when I arrive. I can see him standing over the freshly filled grave. He's staring intently at the gravestone. I park behind Nick's car and turn off the ignition. Nick looks over at me and holds his hand up in a half-wave. His dumb fucking face.

I get out of my car and approach Nick. I say, "Are you sure this is the best idea?"

"Connor Brennan," Nick says.

I say, "Nope. Just me, Candy."

Nick points to the gravestone. "Connor Brennan," he says. "That's Todd's upstairs neighbor."

"I'm sure Todd will enjoy staring at the back of Mr. Brennan's head for all eternity," I say.

"Nah," Nick says. "He's facing down." He chuckles.

"Nick," I say. "Please tell me you're kidding." I say, "You can't bury people upside down, that's just not right!"

Nick shrugs. He says, "He's dead, what does he care?"

I sigh and reach into my back pocket. I hand Nick the

envelope. Nick's eyes flash between my face and the envelope. "What's this?" he says.

"Just open it," I say.

Nick fumbles through the envelope, he eyes the photographs. He reads the note. His stupid fucking smile leaves his face. "Who do you think this is? Who's blackmailing us?"

"His name is Mr. Johnny," I say.

"How do you know that?" Nick asks.

"I don't!" I say. "How the hell am I supposed to know who it is?! I told you this just came in the mail today."

"Jesus," Nick says. "Oh God. What do we do?"

"As much as I hate to say it," I say, "we have to meet this person. We can't just ignore this. They have the knife."

"They *might* have it," Nick says.

"Is it hidden up your ass?" I say. "Because if it's not, then someone else has it. We searched for an hour for that damn thing. And they have pictures of us, Nick. Pictures! We have to talk to them and find out what they want."

Nick doesn't speak for a moment. Then he says, "Okay. Yeah, let's go there."

"Right now?" I ask.

"No," he says. "Tonight." He looks at the gravestone again. "What do you think happened to him?"

"I don't know," I say. "Maybe someone mistook him for someone else and just brutally murdered him? Just like that, 'oops!'" I say, "Do you think that's what happened, Nick?"

Nick says he'll talk to me later. He says, "Let's meet at my place around eight."

—

It's ABOUT SEVEN-THIRTY, and I'm standing in my room in my parent's house, looking at my fat ass. I'm wondering what underwear to wear. I'm thinking about how you shit yourself when you die. I'm wondering which color lipstick would look best in crime scene photos. You have to worry about these things when someone sends you creepy mail with pictures of you. You have to know that no matter what you do you will die one day, and whatever stupid fucking shirt you decided to wear that day would be your ghost outfit shirt forever. Maybe not in a real sense, but you have to know people will see the pictures of your dead body on the internet and they'll say 'Eww! That top does *not* go with that skirt.' All I'm saying is, I'm thinking my ghost ass would have too much cellulite, and for some reason that's the worst thing I can imagine.

My phone rings, it's my mom. She says, "Hey, what are you doing?"

I tell her I'm getting ready to go see Nick.

"I was starting to wonder what happened to him," my mom says. "Well, I was thinking of catching a movie later if you're interested." She asks me when I'll be home.

I'll be surprised if I come home at all.

"Not too late," I say.

"Okay," she says. "Well, let me know if you wanna go to a late one, a movie I mean. We haven't done that in forever."

"Sure thing," I say. "Love you, mom."

"What's that?" she says.

"I love you," I say. I'm getting ready for it.

"Well I love you too," she says. A moment passes and she says, "I was just making sure you knew it was me you were talking to." We get off the phone, and I can't believe my mom's magical ability to turn something good into something bad.

Excuse me if I'm feeling sentimental. I might die tonight.

I finally decide on an outfit. Black and red flannel. Blue jeans. Black Vans. I know what you're thinking: hot shit.

Who knows, maybe this mystery person (Ken, of course it's Ken) is afraid of lumberjacks?

I meet Nick at his house at five after eight. I didn't check the clock, Nick lets me know. Nick looks yellow. Like, Spongebob fuckin' Squarepants yellow.

"Nick," I say. "You gonna be okay?"

"I've just been thinking," he says.

"About your ghost outfit?" I ask.

"What?" he says. "No. I'm just wondering if we should even go. I mean couldn't we come up with something to tell the cops?" He says, "Anything? There has to be another way."

"Well," I say, "I don't know how *hard* you've been thinking, but I wonder if you've thought about the pictures," I say. "Have you thought about the knife? What kind of story could you tell that would clear you of that evidence?"

Nick looks down. "I don't know," he says. "I just don't like where this is going."

"Hey," I say. "You never know. They may have hated Todd, and they want to give us subscriptions to the Jelly of the Month Club."

"What's that?" Nick says.

—

WE ARRIVE at 435 Edgewood Lane at eight-thirty. Yes, I

remember times very well. I also remember the house. It hits me when Nick parks the car. This is where Todd and I screwed. The address didn't mean anything to me, I was never the one who drove here.

Nick asks me what's wrong.

"I'm fine," I say. And I know, typical girl response. This situation is just too complex. I don't know what to say, but I can't back out now.

Nick still hasn't unlocked the car doors. He says, "So, do we just go knock on the door or what?"

"I guess," I say.

He says, "And say what?"

"We say, 'Hi how are ya? We're the folks who you've got pictures of. What's up?" I say.

Nick sighs.

We get out of the car. Nick says, "Hold on," as we reach the mailbox. I'm standing there, female lumberjack, feeling more scared than I could ever let on. Nick fumbles around in the passenger seat. I'm oblivious. I'm wondering if I should have worn the black lipstick instead of the red. Nick returns.

Nick is walking like he's been through the 'special' TSA checkpoint nobody talks about. Gentleman that he is, he lets me lead the way so I don't feel pandered to. I wouldn't want him mansplaining his way all the way up to the top of the stairs. I wouldn't want him thinking I couldn't handle it. There's a point here: he didn't want me to see what was behind his back. Stay with me.

Nick, standing behind me, he says, "Ring the doorbell."

I take a breath and press the doorbell. *Ding-dong.*

A man appears behind the glass in the front door. He holds up a piece of paper. It reads: DOGHOUSE. After we read the note, he walks away.

"Is that some kind of secret code?" Nick says.

"Maybe we should go to the dog house," I say. "I really don't know."

"Yeah," Nick says. "Okay. Let's go to the doghouse. We can play poker with those other dogs. Smoke some cigars." He says, "The painting? You know?"

"'Yeah," I say. "I get it."

Walking down the steps, Nick says, "What if they want us to step onto their property so they can kill us? Say we were coming to attack them?"

"Nick," I say. "First of all, we're already on their property. Secondly, they could have killed us literally any time they wanted to. They watched us bury Todd without us even noticing. I'm pretty sure they don't need us walking into their backyard."

We open the fence leading into the backyard. There is a doghouse in the far-left corner. It looks like a doghouse you would see in a cartoon. It has the typical red roof and everything. Cautiously, we walk over to it.

Nick looks around. He says, "Uh, hey. We're here."

I roll my eyes. I say, "There's a note hanging on it."

Nick tears the paper off of the doghouse. He reads aloud: "Push me."

Getting on the other side of the doghouse, I can't help but smile. "Why do I feel like we're going to some super-secret party?" I say.

"Oh yeah," Nick says. "One where they serve those BTK sandwiches you like so much. The Bind Torture Kill. That one?"

We push the doghouse backwards with ease. There is a dog's water bowl on the ground, except it's not a water bowl at all. The sides look like a typical dog bowl, but in the middle of the 'bowl' is a steering wheel shaped door latch. I grab on each side and turn left until it opens.

"Holy shit," Nick and I say at the same time. The ground parts and a set of stairs appear before us. I decide that since I'm still not dead, I'll play along. We walk down the stairs, and it comes to an opening at the bottom. The doghouse above us slides back over the hole.

We come to a door at the bottom of the stairs, and the intercom next to the door says, "ONE MOMENT PLEASE!"

Nick and I give each other a nervous, adrenaline filled look.

The intercom, it comes back on and a female voice says, "PLEASE PROCEED TO THE END OF THE HALL!" Nick walks in front of me, and for the first time I see it. He's got the Smith & Wesson pistol in the small of his back. We reach the end of the hall when a voice says, "TURN RIGHT AND SIT ON THE COUCH!"

I want to say something about the gun. It's too late now. We sit on the couch as a door on our right opens. Ken Carothers walks into the room. Big shock, I know.

He's wearing a suit and tie. Expensive. He says, "Puts a whole new meaning to sleeping in the doghouse, don't you think?"

Nick, he's sitting in a way that the gun isn't pushed into his back. He's jumpy.

"Look," Ken says. "I know you've got a gun. Make it easier, and just hand it over."

Nick looks shocked. He stands up. "What do you want with us?" He says. "You want revenge for your brother? Forgive me if I want to keep my gun. You're not getting it."

Ken laughs, "That's not your gun, though. Is it? Do you want to hear something funny?"

Nick is sweating bullets.

"The funny thing is," Ken says, "that gun isn't even real. So much of what you know isn't real. Just hand it over, okay? Show me I can trust you."

Nick slowly pulls the gun out from behind his back. He holds the gun in his hands and looks at it. Ken approaches Nick. "There you go," he says. "Not that hard, is it?" Ken reaches for the gun, and Nick points the gun in Ken's face. He tells Ken to back the fuck up.

Ken laughs again. "This is getting ridiculous, kid." He says. "I told you the gun isn't real. Give it over." He holds his hand out.

I'm watching the whole exchange completely clueless of what to do. Nick kind of deserves any punishment he gets for killing Todd, but Ken is a rapist and a murderer. So, there's that.

Understand that I'm not rooting for Ken here. I just don't care enough to get myself killed for Nick.

"You don't understand," Ken says. "And I get that. But I'm not who the media has told you I am. There are a lot of things you don't know, as I've said."

Nick, still pointing the gun at Ken's mug, he says, "I don't believe you. You want to take the gun so you can get rid of us for killing your brother." Nick's voice is shaking.

"Oh my God, you're still on that?" Ken laughs. "Okay," he says. "I was going to wait until you understood more before doing this, but you really need some convincing. It's under-standable." He says, "Todd, will you come here, please?"

Nick looks at me in shock and Ken takes his chance to grab the gun from Nick's hand. For the second time, I see Nick cry.

"Please, don't kill us," he says. "I'm sorry. I'm so sorry for what I did."

The door on the left side of the room opens again. Ken

points the pistol at Nick's face. Todd walks over to where we're standing. He winks at me. He says, "Hey, Candy. Been a while."

Ken pulls the trigger. He says, "BLAM!" Nothing happens. Ken laughs. A warm yellow stream runs out of Nick's pants and onto the floor.

4

KILL 'EM ALL

INSIDE THE DOGHOUSE BUNKER, THINGS ARE GETTING weird. The guy I helped Nick bury is standing right in front of me.

He's dressed nicer than I am.

Todd walks over to a table in the corner of the room and begins digging through vinyl records. Nick is looking down at the mess he made on the floor.

Ken says, "I was very impressed with the way you two handled the situation *this one* got you into," he points at Nick.

Me, I'm the type of person who has to know how a card trick is done, especially if it was very good.

I say, "You have to tell me what's going on. How is Todd still here? I tossed his body into an empty grave. I saw him full of holes. He was dead as shit."

"If you tell me why you tried to kill him," Ken says. "I'll tell you more."

"She didn't try to kill anyone," Nick says. "I was trying to kill *you.*"

"But she helped you cover it up," Ken says. "Isn't that right?"

"Yeah," I say. "At least I thought I did."

From the corner of the room, Metallica begins to play.

"Tell me, Nick," Ken says. "What made you want to kill me?"

"I heard about what you did," Nick says. "Anyone who could do what you did deserves to die."

"And how do you know what I did?" Ken says.

Nick, getting annoyed, he says, "Because it was on the fucking five-o-clock news! Because everyone knows what you did!"

"Oh, okay." Ken says. "So, you believe everything the media tells you. That's great. And here I was thinking you might actually be the ones we needed."

James Hetfield is saying to hit the lights.

"Oh, fuck you," Nick says. "Jet fuel doesn't melt steel beams, either. Do you really expect me to believe you're innocent?"

"I honestly don't care if you believe me or not, as long as you understand what's going to happen," Ken says. "You're going to do what we ask of you, when we ask it. You'll be compensated well, but you absolutely will do what we say, with no questions asked."

"And what if we don't do what you say?" Nick asks. "You gonna kill us?"

"I won't have to kill you," Ken says. "I've got photo-graphic evidence. Did you forget that?"

Nick is silent. I hadn't forgotten, though. It's all I can think about.

"Also, we've got this now," Ken says. "Play it, Todd."

Todd turns down the volume on the record player and picks up a small remote. He presses a button on the remote, and my voice plays through the bunker's loudspeakers: "How is Todd still here?" My voice says. "I tossed his body into an empty grave. I saw him full of holes."

Ken smiles. He says, "It's really a nice little package just ready and waiting to be sent to the cops."

—

KEN POINTS to a doorway to his left. He says, "Through this door, you will find your quarters. You may shower, change clothes, get comfortable." Nick looks at me with a look of total confusion.

"He's serious," Todd says. "Go for it. We'll be waiting."

Nick, he's pissed himself, my pants are too tight, and these people have a taped confession from me. I decide to take the damn shower.

Nick and I go through the door, and we find ourselves in another hallway, this one with multiple doors.

"Bathrooms are on the left," Ken says. "The doors are labeled."

Ken steps back through the doorway, saying, "We will be waiting out here to talk."

Nick looks over at me. "What are we going to do?" he says.

I'm thinking of the phrase, *you will be compensated well.* I'm thinking of prison. "I don't know what choice we really have," I say. "I guess we have to hear them out."

As I strip down in the women's room, I can't help but wonder if I'm being recorded. I probably am. I'm beginning to ask myself why it is that I don't even care.

The water comes from the overhead shower and it stings my skin. As I run my fingers through my hair, I'm wondering how I managed to find myself in this predicament. But then my mind says, *because you didn't report Nick immediately. You know why you're here.*

After I'm finished showering, I dry off with a towel I find hanging outside the shower door. There is a box sitting in a chair on the far side of the room. In marker, written on the side of the box in the same handwriting found on the package I received at my house—the one with the photographs of me—is my name. I go to the chair and open the box.

—

I ENTER the hallway and see that Nick is already waiting for me. He's wearing a suit, complete with a tie. He's wearing the fanciest men's shoes I've ever seen. He looks like a poor man's (or rather, woman's) Matthew McConaughey. It's actually amazing what some nice clothes do for Nick's look.

Nick looks me up and down. He sees my red Terani Couture cocktail dress. His eyes work their way down my body, and he sees my Charlotte Olympia Irina platform sandals. "Damn," Nick says. It's weird seeing him looking at me like this. I've never been looked at like this in my life.

The door at the end of the hall opens, and Ken asks us to please join him in the conference room. As we walk down the hall—and I'm doing my best impression of someone who can actually walk in high-heels—I can't help imagining rolling my ankle so hard that my bone pops out the other side.

We follow Ken into what he calls the conference room. The air has a stale quality, reminding me of a car that's been locked shut for a month. That, or Nick's bedroom. Ken gestures toward two chairs sitting on the far side of a table. Nick and I take our seats. The room is cold and empty, save for the table and chairs.

Ken sits across from us. "Todd," he calls. "Todd, come here." Ken looks at me and flashes a smile. "Brothers," he says with a sigh.

Todd enters the room and takes the seat next to Ken. He leans over to whisper something in Ken's ear. To my surprise, Ken backs away from Todd. "Whatever you have to say," Ken says, "I'm quite sure you can say it in front of the whole class."

"I don't—" Todd says, but Ken cuts him off.

"Say what you need to say, or leave," he says.

I can't believe the exchange I'm watching.

"Fine," Todd says. "The news says they've found you. They say there is a chase, and it's on TV."

"This is great news," Ken says. "The best news. I hope they kill me."

Todd presses a button on the wall, and a television screen descends from the ceiling. He pulls a remote out of his pocket and presses a few buttons until the news is playing on the flat screen. Half a dozen police cars are chasing a blue Dodge Dart. The reporter is saying how the manhunt for rapist and murderer, Ken Carothers, of Grand Rapids, Michigan, was about to be over, finally. Ken's mugshot is in the top-left corner of the screen.

Ken sits across from me and laughs like a stoner binging

Family Guy. He turns to me and says, "I don't expect you to get why this is so funny, but trust me, it's classic stuff."

On the TV screen, the police corner the Dodge. The cops get out of their cars, and all of them have their guns pointed at the man the news is calling Ken Carothers.

Then, the Ken in the same room as me, he says, "Here we go." The four of us watch as the man steps out of his Dodge Dart and tries to jump over the side of the bridge he's parked on. We watch as he's filled full of bullets; we watch his body fall on the ground. Ken and Todd begin to cheer and high-five each other.

—

TODD TURNS OFF THE TV. He turns and sits next to Ken.

"It's time to tell us what's going on," Nick says. "No more bullshit."

"Did you miss the part," Ken says, "where I said 'no questions asked?'"

Before Nick can reply, Ken continues, "I'll tell you as much as I can, for now. Only because I need your cooperation, and I believe that will come a lot easier if you don't think of me as a rapist."

Nick and I sit in silence.

"When Todd and I were young, we were used in. . . experiments. Our parents participating in a government program, not realizing what it entailed. They were told that we would have blood drawn, and that we would be held overnight. That was all. There was *a lot* of money involved, which is why they took the bait. They figured, what government would intentionally harm kids?"

I'm thinking of Project MKUltra. I'm thinking of child pedophile rings.

Ken continues, "They took me first, when I was very young. Todd was taken when I was fifteen years old. They told our parents that they were studying genetics. They said that my parents' cooperation could save thousands of lives."

"What were they really doing?" I say.

"Studying serial killers," Ken says. "They wanted to study the effects of upbringing and environment in the early stages of development. Of course, in order to do that, they had to have a constant and a variable."

"So, they cloned us," Todd says.

Now, forgive me if I just take what Todd and Ken are saying with a grain of salt. I've seen both of them dead already.

"So," I say. "The little girl. . . that wasn't you who raped and killed her?"

"Nope," Ken says. "I've been watching everything play out safely down here."

"How do we know you're not the one who *did* do those things?" Nick asks.

"You don't," Ken says. "But that's the least of your worries."

"Why is that?" Nick says.

"Because this organization who did this to Todd and me," Ken says, "they got a little ambitious in their studies."

"They've been doing this a long time," Todd says.

"That's right," Ken says. "And someone thought it would be a good idea to clone some of the country's most notorious serial killers. Raising them in totally different ways, trying to see if their brains were the cause, or their upbringing, you see. The experiment was a success, and now the government has trained killers. Trained *serial killers*. The worst part? They don't even know who or *what* they are. Many of them are living regular lives."

"What are they using them for?" Nick asks. "You say they don't know who or what they are, what good are they then? They sound harmless."

"They can be activated whenever they are needed. They've done it already."

"What are they using them for?" I say.

"As far as we can tell," Ken says. "They intended on using them for government business. *Taking out the trash,* I guess you could say. It's the perfect scapegoat. They get these guys, they change their look, and they can order a hit on anyone they want, any time they want. They're positioned all over the country, and they're doing what serial killers do best."

"Where are you getting all of this information?" Nick says. "And what's the deal with the high-tech bunker?"

"That's 'need to know' information," Ken says. "And you don't need to know."

"Well," I say, "can I at least ask what the deal is with the fancy clothes? What do you need from us?"

"After we saw what you two did with Todd's clone, we figured you'd be the best candidates to help us with what we need," Ken says. "The clothes," he says, "are to keep up appearances." He hands me a manila folder. "You've got two first class tickets to Florida."

"What's in Florida?" Nick asks.

Ken leans back in his chair. He looks at Todd. They both say in unison: "Ted Bundy."

5

THE NUMBER OF THE BEAST

IN THE FIRST-CLASS SECTION OF A BOEING 777, IT'S EASY TO forget that I'm not some rich bitch on vacation. The alcohol helps. That's another thing: Ken provided Nick and I with fake ID's.

Me, I'm Heather Wolworth. My parents own a line of fancy hotels. Nick, he's Benjamin Clancy, Heather Wolworth's pretentious boyfriend. Benjamin's daddy owns four yachts.

The stewardess who takes my drink order, she stands around after bringing the first round like she's waiting for an autograph. Nick pulls a ten-dollar bill out of his shirt pocket and slips it to the woman. This is what rich feels like. Always getting the best service. When I go out to eat with my parents at Applebee's, we can't even get refills for our water.

Nick is playing some game on his phone. A little stick figure man stands in the center of the screen, and Nick has to find new and better ways to kill him each time. In my mind, I wonder if there's a universe where stick figure people find different ways to kill humans.

"So," Nick says, "being rich is awesome."

"We're not rich," I say.

"Sure we are," Nick says. "As long as we do what they say, we'll never have to worry about money."

The stewardess returns. She's brought us our second round of drinks, and the plane hasn't even left the ground. Nick and I take the drinks from her, and she stands there once again, staring. I smile up at her and say, "Thanks." I begin talking to Nick about all the sights we absolutely *must* see in Florida. I'm using my best I-come-from-money voice. The stewardess, she walks away looking annoyed.

Once she's gone, I say, "And what is it, exactly, that they will ask us to do? What makes you so sure it's something you'd be willing to do?"

"What makes me sure," Nick says, taking a sip of his second martini in the past fifteen minutes, "is the fact that the opportunity has fallen in our lap to do what we've always wanted. To do what Dexter did. And in Florida to boot." He chuckles. "Come on, Candy," he says. "We are perfect for this."

"This is never what I wanted," I say. "You're happy about this because you got lucky."

Nick returns to his game. He sighs.

I'm looking out the window as the captain comes over the intercom and tells us that we are about to take off. The captain says how we are expected to land in Tallahassee in about three-and-a-half hours.

We don't talk much on the flight. I'm reading a book called *House of the Holy,* by a guy named James F. Goffio and trying not to lose my shit internally. I've got too much on my mind. It's driving me crazy just how *okay* Nick is with all of this. He's actually *excited* to kill people.

The captain comes over the intercom again. "We will be

landing shortly," he says. "We want to thank you for choosing Delta Airlines."

Nick turns to me and says, "Have you ever wondered what it's like to die in a plane crash?"

"Your timing is awful," I say.

"Yeah, but have you?" he asks.

"Of course I have," I say. "And I'd rather not think about it now." The plane rocks.

"I just wonder what it feels like to fall from thousands of feet in the air, the whole time knowing you're about to die horrifically." Nick shivers.

The brochure sticking out of the back of the seat in front of me reads: First Class: Fly in Complete Comfort. If they really want me to be comfortable, someone should remove Nick from my immediate vicinity.

As the plane begins its descent, Nick makes crashing sounds with his mouth.

—

NICK and I gather our luggage and follow the signs to the taxi pickup spot outside. Scanning the signs, I find the one with the name WOLWORTH in big, black letters. Nick and I approach the man holding the sign, and his nametag says his name is Felix.

"Hi, Felix," I say. "I'm . . ." I struggle to remember my name. "I'm Heather," I say. "Heather Wolworth." Felix takes my hand and holds it between his palms.

"Very pleased to meet you," he says. "Where are we going today?"

I pull the card out of my purse, the card with Ken's instructions. "Hotel Duval," I say.

Felix nods and leads us to the back of the limousine.

"So, what now?" Nick says in the back of the limo.

"All Ken said was to go to the room," I say. "Maybe we'll find out more then."

The little window between us and the driver slowly descends. "So," Felix says, "what brings you to the capital of Florida?"

"Vacation," I say.

"Forgive me for saying so, ma'am," Felix says. "But if I was going to vacation in Florida, I think I'd pick somewhere with a beach." He chuckles.

"She's terrified of beaches," Nick says. "Her uncle was eaten alive by a shark when she was five years old. Happened right in front of her. She can't even watch the movie *Jaws* without screaming like a baby."

"Oh, that's terrible!" Felix says, as he turns the limo.

"Yeah," I say, flashing an angry look at Nick. "It's a wonder I ended up with a guy who's in the yacht business. Sometimes I think it might have been a mistake." Felix chuckles again.

"Well," he says, "you picked a pretty safe spot to vacation then, I'd say. Just stay away from the swamps. There's gators out there that could give old Jaws a run for his money."

Felix stops the limo. "Hotel Duval," he says. "It's been a pleasure driving you."

We check in to the hotel with no problems, using my fake ID. The hostess at the front counter lets me know that we've got the biggest suite in the Duval. The girl asks if we need help with our bags.

"Oh, no. Thank you," I say. We only have two small bags.

We turn to enter the elevator and a small man whose nametag reads: CLARENCE stops us.

"Let me take your bags," Clarence says.

I wave him off. "No thanks," I say. "We've got it. My boyfriend, Benjamin, has really weak arms, he could use the workout." Nick turns red.

"I insist," Clarence says, as he grabs our bags and steps into the elevator. Clarence leads us to our room and instructs me to swipe my card. The door opens, and Clarence sets our bags on the table inside the door.

"Thank you," Nick says. Clarence stands there in the hallway, hand outstretched. Nick reaches into his pocket to tip Clarence.

We shut the door to the hotel suite. There is a box sitting on the enormous bed in the center of the room. Nick and I open the box and begin laying the contents out on the bed. Inside there are knives, two handguns, two cellphones, a car key, and some folders.

Nick picks up the first folder and begins reading aloud: "Welcome, initiates. We hope the suite is a symbol of our commitment to your utmost comfort and luxury during your employment with us. You will need to destroy your old phones. In the new phones, you will find all the contacts you will need pre-loaded."

While Nick is talking, I'm opening the second folder.

"After you have settled in," Nick continues, "you will need to begin work as soon as possible. Your first job is detailed in the second folder. You will find an address, along with a photograph with a description and pertinent details. It is essential that you get started immediately. The subject is very dangerous; a ticking time bomb. After the job is done, call 'Mr. Z' in the phone provided for you. Good luck."

Nick sets down the paper and smiles. "This is good stuff," he says. "I feel so important, like a secret agent."

Holding the photo up, I say, "This doesn't look like Ted Bundy at all." The man in the photo has a shaved head and a goatee. "He looks more like Heisenberg."

"Well, they said they changed their appearances," Nick says. "I expected him to look different." Nick takes the photo from me.

"Don Branson," he says. "666 Waterloo Avenue."

"Did you seriously just say six-six-six Waterloo?" I ask.

"Yup," he says, chuckling. "Hail Satan!"

—

AFTER CHANGING clothes and concealing our weapons, Nick and I take the elevator to the lobby. The hostess at the front desk doesn't look up, and I'm glad because we look very different than when we arrived. Miss Heather Wolworth is now plain old Candy Tran. Mr. Benjamin Clancy is now just Nick Ford. We're just two dumbass kids in way over their heads.

We stop outside, and Nick presses the PANIC button on the car's key fob. A black Camaro begins to scream on the far side of the parking lot.

"I'm driving," Nick says. I tell him to knock himself out. I feel like I'm going to be sick. But for us, it's kill or be killed. Or worse, jailed for life.

Nick cranks the car, and I'm looking at the profile of Don Branson, the supposed Ted Bundy clone. Don has a wife and three little girls. He works at Florida State University. He is a deacon at his Methodist church.

On the radio, Iron Maiden sing *666, the number of the beast. Hell and fire was spawned to be released.*

"I know you're going to chicken out," Nick says. "And I just want you to know you don't have to worry. I got this. I mean, can you imagine? I get to kill *Ted Bundy*."

"Don Branson," I say. "And who says I'm going to chicken out? I've made it this far!"

"We haven't even done anything yet," he says. "I know how you feel about all of this."

"Nick," I say, "why are you okay with all of it?"

Nick glances at the GPS, turns the car left, and says, "this is what I was meant to do. Can't you feel it?"

I can't.

The GPS announces that we have arrived at our destination. It has just turned dark outside, and we can see shadows moving inside the house.

"We can't do this," I say. "His whole family is here. He has kids. This isn't right."

"Candy," he says, "this is what I was talking about. You'll thank me after this is over. You'll thank me when you get your money, and more importantly, when you don't go to prison."

"We could go to prison for *this crime,*" I say.

Nick sighs. "You're being a real Debbie Downer," he says. And before I can stop him, he gets out of the car.

Nick walks briskly up the driveway. He reaches into his back pocket and pulls out a black ski mask.

Oh shit, I'm thinking. *This is real.*

I start to panic as Nick reaches to ring the doorbell. I honk the Camaro's horn. Nick throws his hands up and turns around, furious.

I have to stop this. I'm thinking. *I can't let him do this.* I get out of the car and run towards the front door. "Nick!" I'm saying. "Nick, let's go, this is crazy!"

Raised voices come from inside the house. Nick dives into the bushes by the front door like the world's lamest prankster. And when the door swings open, I'm standing face to face with Don Branson. For a few moments, we just stare. Don looks at my outfit. He sees the handgun tucked into my waistband.

"I knew you'd come eventually," he says. He's reaching slowly behind him.

"I'm leaving," I say, my voice shaking. "This is a misunderstanding."

I start backing away from Don's porch, eyes never leaving his.

A woman's voice comes from behind Don. "Who's out there, Donnie?" she says.

Tears in my eyes, I'm shaking my head. My hands are up as I continue to back towards the Camaro. At this point, if I reach the car alive, I'm leaving Nick in the goddamn bushes.

On his front porch, Don Branson pulls a pistol from behind his back and aims it at me. Don's wife screams when she comes outside.

I turn to run and wait for death. I'm wondering how bad it will hurt when the bullet tears through my body.

Don Branson's wife screams louder when Nick shoots from the bushes, and Don's brains splatter the front of her dress.

6

PETE'S GIFT SHOP

I DON'T KNOW WHY I'M SURPRISED. I KNEW WHAT WE WERE going to do when Nick and I got in the car, but it doesn't make me feel any better. So, this guy is the supposed clone of Ted Bundy. According to Ken and Todd, he's a government plant with a vicious internal bloodlust. Right now, he's just a guy on his porch with a second asshole in his forehead.

The wife, she's passed out in the doorway. "Come on!" I shout. Nick has left his spot in the bushes and is standing over Don Branson's limp body. He bends down and reaches into the dead guy's pocket.

"What the hell are you doing?" I ask. I'm backed all the way against the Camaro now, and I'm tempted to just open the door and drive. Only problem is: Nick has the keys.

I look up at the porch and see Nick standing over Don's wife now. He's aiming the pistol at her head. "No!" I'm screaming, running towards Nick.

Nick turns and looks at me. With his ski mask on, it's a lot easier to forget that he's my boyfriend. It makes it easier to forget that I've *slept with him*. It also makes it easier to remember that I hate him.

"What is your problem?" Nick asks. He swings the gun around, nearly pointing at it my head.

"My problem is," I say, "we're done here. The guy is dead. We don't need to kill her, too." I point to the unconscious woman lying in her husband's blood.

Nick looks at me with eyes that stare into my soul. "We're going to miss *Rick and Morty*," he says.

"What?" is all I can manage.

"If we take too long," Nick says. "It comes on at eleven."

"Come on," I say. "Let's go!"

"Let's get him in the car," Nick says. "We need to dispose of the evidence."

"The evidence? What about the blood? There's evidence all over the garden gnomes!" I say.

"I'm pretty sure Ken doesn't want us leaving the body of Ted Bundy's clone here for the cops to find," Nick says. "Call me crazy."

"You're crazy," I say.

Two minutes later, Don Branson is in the trunk of the Camaro. Nick starts walking up toward the house.

"What are you doing?" I say.

"She saw you, Candy," Nick says.

"First of all," I say, "I'm not Candy. I'm Heather Wolworth. Candy would never be a part of this bullshit. And secondly, I don't care. We're completely random here. She saw me for like half a second. She doesn't need to die, too!"

Nick considers this. He looks like someone who can't decide if he wants to upsize his meal to a large or not. "But," he says. But then we hear the sirens. At this point, it's the only thing saving Mr. Branson's widow.

We get in the car, and Nick lets out a moan. As we drive

away, we pass a black van parked on the other side of the road. It would be much later before I realized the significance of that van.

—

NICK DIALS the number for the contact called "Mr. Z," and the phone starts ringing through the speakers in the car. My head is killing me, and I'm trying not to cry.

Someone on the other end of the phone answers: "Is it done?" the voice says in a robotic grumble.

"Yeah," Nick says. "He's dead. Dead as shit. I—"

"And were there witnesses?" the voice says. Nick shoots a look in my direction. My palms are sweaty. I reach to turn down the A/C.

Nick hesitates. Finally, he says, "No witnesses."

"Very good," the voice says. "And the body?"

"Yeah," Nick says. "We weren't sure what to do about that. Do you guys have like a chop-shop or something?"

There is a pause at the other end of the line. Then, Mr. Z says, "Just eliminate the body."

"Of course," Nick says. "Yeah, no problem."

"You will find the funds in your accounts by the morning. I will contact you with your next location." And before the man hangs up, he says, "You did a good thing."

Nick pulls the Camaro into an IHOP parking lot.

"What are we doing?" I say, curling my hair around my finger. I'm jonesing for a cigarette, and I don't even smoke.

"We're getting something to eat while we think about what to do next," Nick says.

"I don't think that's a great idea, Nick. We need to get rid of this guy."

—

"WHAT'LL IT BE, SWEETIE?" says a waitress in a blue smock. The whole place smells like coffee and failure. Nick speaks for me.

"She'll have the French toast. It's her favorite. Right, babe?" he says.

"Um," I say, thinking I couldn't eat if Pamela here held a gun to my head. "Yeah, sure."

"I'll have a bacon cheeseburger and fries," Nick says. "And two coffees."

The waitress smiles. "Coming right up," she says.

If you didn't already think Nick was a monster, I'd just like to remind you that he ordered a *bacon cheeseburger* from the International House of Pancakes.

"So," Nick says. "Got any ideas? About the body?"

"Oh, I'm glad you specified what you were referring to, Nick," I say. "Not sure I would have understood you otherwise."

Nick glares at me from across the table. Veins stick out on his forehead. "You know what?" he says. "I can't believe you're giving *me* shit right now. After what you did. You heard what Mr. Z said about witnesses. But no, you wouldn't let me finish the job."

"You know what I think, Nick?" I say. "I think you oughta call Mr. Z and ask if he'd like his dick su—"

"Two coffees," the waitress says. It's as if she was tele-ported to our table from a tube in the floor.

"Thanks," Nick mutters. Considering we're not currently Heather Wolworth and Benjamin Clancy, I'm thinking those drinks came pretty goddamn fast.

Pamela walks away again, and Nick begins to drink his coffee hot and black. Once again, what a fucking unforgiv-able, relentless monster.

A family walks in and is seated at a table across the room. The whole family is sunburnt. All of them are wearing FSU gear, and it's not even football season. If Tallahassee gets tourists, they enjoy IHOP for their late-night dinner needs. The youngest boy is wearing a shirt with a cartoon alligator on the front. The bold letters read: I GOT MY PICTURE WITH GARY THE GATOR. And below that: PETE'S GIFT SHOP.

"Nick," I say. "Unfortunately, I have an idea."

—

NICK DRIVES, and I give directions. "It says here that the shop closes at nine on weeknights," I say, looking at my phone. It's five after nine.

"Perfect," Nick says. He's tapping the steering wheel to the beat of some shitty radio rock song. He looks like a teenage boy who just touched a boob for the first time in his life.

"Is this enjoyable for you?" I ask.

"It's not for you? We're taking out the trash, Candy. Come on."

I don't answer.

We arrive at Pete's Gift Shop ten minutes later. The parking lot is empty. "Where's this gator?" Nick says, peering into the glass window up front.

I walk around to the side of the building using a stone walking path. "Over here," I say. "They keep him outside." There's a fenced-in area on the right side of the building. It's a very small area for an animal Gary's size, no bigger than a ten-by-twenty-foot dog fence. There are feet painted on the ground in front of the fence where tourists can snap pictures with Gary's cage.

I can see the gator sitting in the back corner of his habitat. He's watching us intently. I'm wondering how well-fed he is.

"How are we going to do this?" I say.

"It was your idea," Nick says. "You tell me."

Rolling my eyes, I say, "Well, I'm not getting my ass in there with him. Are you?"

"Nope," Nick says.

"So, then we just... I guess we just throw him over." I say.

Nick and I open the trunk of the Camaro and pull out the body of Don Branson. What they say about the dead passing gas is true. When that trunk opens, it's like a visceral punch to the olfactory senses. My eyes water, and I try not to puke.

"Son of a bitch," Nick says. "Smells like a battleshits tournament in a Taco Bell bathroom in there."

"Maybe Gary likes 'em smelly," I say. "Like when catfish go after chicken livers."

Nick and I haul Don's heavy ass to the fence and try to swing him over the side. We fail horribly, and Don bounces off the fence and flops on the ground. Gary makes hissing noises and moves closer.

"He's too heavy," I say.

"Nah, we can do it," Nick says. "We just have to go about it differently."

We push Don's body against the fence and begin rolling him upward, shifting his weight around. Finally, we are able to clear the top of the fence, and Don's body hits the ground with a thud. Gary the gator backs away at first, but then, after a moment, he descends on the body, ripping and tearing, clothes and all.

"They must keep him starved," Nick says.

"Yeah," I say. "Lucky for us."

—

AN HOUR LATER, we arrive back at the hotel. Surprisingly enough, neither of us have any blood on us. We walk past the receptionist, and I'm glad the shift change occurred. We look completely different than the rich kids who checked in this morning.

When we enter the room, the first thing Nick does is turn on the TV. "Sweet," he says. "*Rick and Morty* is about to start."

We just hand fed Don Branson to Gary the gator, and Nick is worried about missing a cartoon.

"I'm taking a shower," I say. It's too bad I can't give my mind a shower. I can't stop thinking about Don's head exploding like a rotten pumpkin.

I'm not used to fancy hotels, and I'm a little blown away by the bathroom of the Hotel Duval. I've seen motor homes smaller than this bathroom. The shower feels amazing, of course. But as I'm washing my hair, I hear a grumbling noise. I know it's the water pooling and being sucked down the drain, but in the back of my mind, I'm picturing Gary sitting in the corner of the shower, waiting for seconds. When the soap is clear of my eyes, I look down and scream in shock. Bloody water is pooled around my feet.

"You okay?" Nick says from the other side of the door.

"Yeah," I say. "It's nothing."

On top of everything else, I've started my period.

—

WHEN I LEAVE THE BATHROOM, I find Nick sprawled on the bed, snoring. The suite is massive, and I'm not sleeping with Nick—not tonight. There are two other beds, I'll gladly take either. Maybe even lock the door. And I know I'm a part of this, too, but it doesn't make me feel better about what I've seen Nick do. The way he can just kill with no remorse.

I pick the bedroom on the left side of the suite and close the door, locking it behind me. After watching a few minutes of *The Golden Girls,* I drift off to sleep.

Dorothy, Rose, Blanche, and Sophia gather around my hotel bed. They all smile at me, but there is a look of concern in their eyes.

"What have you got yourself into now, hon?" Rose asks, arms folded.

"Oh, leave her alone," Sophia says. "She didn't know it would get this bad. What was she supposed to do?"

I try to speak but find myself unable to.

"I think she's trying to impress that boy," Blanche says. "What was his name?"

"Todd?" Dorothy says. "He is a cutie. And so dapper!"

A phone rings in the corner of the room, and Rose walks over to it. Picking up the receiver, she listens and nods. "That's no surprise," she says. She hangs up the phone and turns to me. "It's for you," she says.

I wake up in a pool of sweat and my cellphone is ringing. Mr. Z is the caller. I stand up and quickly run into the room where Nick was sawing logs earlier. Nick isn't there. I glance down at the phone again, and apprehensively, I answer.

"H-hello?" I say.

"Where are you, right now?" the jumbled voice says.

"I'm in the Hotel. The Duval. Why?" I say.

There is a moment of silence. "Do you know where Nick is?" the voice asks.

"He was sleeping," I say. "He was in the room."

"Turn on the news," the voice demands.

I fumble for the remote. "What's going on?" I ask, flipping through the channels. But then I see it. The headline reads: **Police in search of Estelle Branson's killer**. I turn up the volume.

"Mere hours after the murder of a Tallahassee man, Don Branson, his wife, Estelle, has been shot and killed. Police received a phone call when a neighbor noticed a black Camaro parked at the Branson house, the same one that was reportedly seen leaving after Mr. Branson's murder."

"Candy," Mr. Z says. My phone beeps. I look down and see: Nick calling.

7

HEY JUDE

IF YOU HAVEN'T FIGURED IT OUT BY NOW, NICK IS BECOMING A problem for me. Mr. Z sighs impatiently and asks who is calling me.

"Nick," I say. "He's on the other line."

"You can call him back," the man says. "But you should know that he is becoming a bit of a liability for you. You cannot afford to be caught."

"I know," I say. "Can't I just ditch him?"

"Just control him better," he says. "Call me back after you meet with him." And he hangs up the phone.

Pacing around the hotel suite, I dial Nick's number. The phone rings twice before Nick answers. "Hello?" he says.

"You're famous," I say.

"Yeah. About that," he says. "I screwed up, Candy. Someone saw me."

"What the hell were you thinking?" I ask. I can hear the sound of the Camaro's engine roaring in the background.

Nick sighs. "I was trying to tie up the loose ends," he says. "Mr. Z said—"

"Mr. Z is pissed," I say. "Where are you now?"

"I'm almost back to the hotel," he says.

"No!" I shout. Realizing I'm in a fancy hotel full of people, I lower my voice. "You can't come back here," I say. "It's too risky. We need to meet somewhere else."

"How about the IHOP?" Nick says. I pause for a whole minute. I want to tell Nick that he's an idiot for thinking of that. I want to, but I'm starving.

—

I'M SITTING across from Nick in the International House of Pancakes in the same booth we were sitting in mere hours ago. Luckily, just like the hotel, there has been a shift change, and none of the staff notices us. A dusty hag with skin like a pair of leather boots takes our order, and Nick drinks his coffee black.

Once the waitress is gone, I look at Nick and say, "We have to call Mr. Z. He's going to tell us what to do next. Maybe, if we're lucky, he can get us out of this mess."

"I was only doing what he said," Nick says. "And you know it."

"How could you think it was a good idea to return to a crime scene?" I ask. "Can you really be that stupid?"

Nick looks down at the coffee the same color of his soul. "Well," he says, "I think I've heard enough bitching at the moment. If you don't mind, I'm gonna take a piss. You can think about how I saved us until I get back. Then we can call him."

"Bitching?" I say. "Who's bitching? I'm just being realistic!"

"Oh. Right. I forgot that you're sweet, innocent Candy. So fucking sweet I might get diabetes just being so close to you," Nick says. He walks to the bathroom.

Fuming, I sip my stale coffee. I had left the hotel room in a haste, walking the two blocks to the IHOP and shoving all of my things into the back of the Camaro. I didn't notice the black van following me then, either.

The food comes, and Nick still hasn't returned. I pick up my phone and try to call him. It rings until it goes through to voicemail. At this point, Nick has been gone almost ten minutes.

"Is everything okay?" the waitress asks, refilling our coffee pitcher.

"Oh, yeah," I say. "Food's great." But I know that isn't what she means. What she means is *where the fuck is your boyfriend?* I wish I knew.

"You know," she says, "I had this happen to me once."

"Oh yeah?" I say. "What's that?"

"My date ditched me in a restaurant. Climbed out the bathroom window. Or, well, he *tried* to climb out the bathroom window. Ended up getting stuck and they had to call emergency crews to get him out." The woman giggles. "You can imagine how shitty that made me feel, thinking that this guy would rather climb out of a window than just finish our date. But it was pretty funny watching everyone take pictures of his flailing legs," she says. "But anyways," she says, "you may want to check. Just to be sure."

"Check the men's room to make sure my boyfriend hasn't left out a window?" I ask.

"That's right," the waitress says. And with a wink, she's gone.

Tapping my nails on the table, another minute goes by. Suddenly, like a jack-in-the-box, I shoot up out of my seat and storm to the bathrooms. I knock on the men's room door. A crashing sound comes from inside. I push the door open violently and see blood streaking the floor and countertop. The trail of blood leads into the handicapped stall on the far side of the room.

"Who's in here?" A gruff voice barks. I freeze, silent. I can hear choking sounds and water splashing. After a few moments, the torture continues.

"I won't ask you again, motherfucker," the man says. "The next time you make me ask, I'll cut your throat and let you bleed out in this Waffle House bathroom. Now, who sent you?"

As carefully as I can, I slowly reach behind me and pull the pistol from the small of my back. I have no idea what I intend to do with it, but it happens so fast, and it just feels like the only option I have.

Over the speakers in the ceiling, The Beatles are singing, *na na na na na na na, na na na na, hey Jude.*

Nick is making harsh choking sounds, no more, no less. It's pathetic, but I feel bad for him. I walk over to the stall and swing open the door. "Hey asshole," I say. The monster of a man in the blue suit turns around. He's holding a knife. "It's an IHOP bathroom." I'm pointing the gun at him, and he doesn't seem the least bit scared.

"What the fuck are you talking about?" The man says in a Jersey Shore accent. His slicked back hair makes him look like an over-inflated toddler on picture day.

"The bathroom," I say. "You said it was a Waffle House. This is an IHOP."

The man laughs. "Listen at this cunt," he says. And before he can say another word, I hit him as hard as I can between the eyes with the butt of the pistol. Nick looks up at me. "Thanks," he says, his head and torso soaked in toilet water and blood. His nose is broken.

"We need to go," I say. "Come on, get up."

The large man is lying prone on the floor.

"He ambushed me," Nick says. "Slammed my face on the bathroom counter. I'm gonna kill him."

"You've done enough killing," I say. "Grab his wallet, and let's go before someone finds us in here."

Nick fishes the man's wallet out of his pants pocket and grabs his knife. Luckily, there's an emergency exit right outside the bathroom door. We push open the door and climb into the Camaro.

"We didn't pay the bill," Nick says.

"Yep," I say. "I think that's the least of our worries."

I start the car and back out of the spot quickly. "Call Mr. Z," I say. "Tell him we're in trouble." Nick turns down the A/C, shivering. He smells like piss. I drive the car out of the parking lot, driving towards anywhere else.

Nick dials the number and puts the phone on speaker.

"Yes," says the low voice of the man called Mr. Z.

"We're on the road," Nick says. "Someone just tried to kill me in an IHOP bathroom. That make any sense to you?"

"Can you give me a description?" Mr. Z says.

"I can do better than that," Nick says, fumbling through the wallet. He pulls out a driver's license. "The name on his license is George Kazinski."

"You got his license? Is he dead?" Mr. Z says, sounding like he's hiding excitement.

"No," I say. "I knocked him out, and we left him."

"Ahh, Candy," the man says. "And how are you this evening?"

"Fucking swell," I say.

"Well," Mr. Z says. "I believe you will wish you'd killed him."

"Who is he?" Nick says.

"Can't tell you that," says the man. "But I can tell you one thing. He wasn't the only one. Keep your eyes peeled. They may even be following you right now."

I shoot a nervous glance towards the rear-view mirror. Nothing so far.

"Now," Mr. Z says. "Your next target is in New Orleans. I did have a flight booked for the morning, but I'm going to have to ask you to drive. Keep moving. And if you notice someone following you—"

The back windshield explodes inward as a spray of bullets peppers the Camaro.

"Fuck!" Nick screams, dropping the phone.

"Hello?" Mr. Z says. "What was that?"

I'm struggling like hell to keep the car on the road. Ducking my head, it's hard to keep the car from swerving. "We're being shot at!" Nick screams as he climbs into the backseat. He lies down long ways and chambers a round in his pistol.

"What kind of vehicle is it?" The phone on the floor-board says.

Nick pops his head up. "Black van," he says. "Shit!" More bullets. I swerve the car hard, almost losing control.

"Come on, Nick," I say. "You need to do *something.*"

Nick pops his hand up over the back of the seat and begins returning fire. The sound is deafening in the little car. With every *pop*, my body grows more tense. My heart is beating so hard and I'm trying not to vomit the coffee I drank down the front of my shirt.

More bullets. This time one of the bullets hits the head-rest where Nick was sitting, blowing a hole through it. There is no one else on this dark road at this time of night. I'd even take police right now. I think.

In the confusion, I'd forgotten about Mr. Z, until I heard him say *this won't work if they die,* in a hushed voice. A second voice mumbled something, but I couldn't hear what it said.

Nick fires more rounds. This time he had popped his head up and taken good aim. "I got one of the headlights!" he says. I could see in my mirrors that the van was speeding up, coming up on our left.

"You get ready to get this bastard," I say.

"Got it," Nick says. I hear the gun cock again as Nick loads a second magazine.

"Are you ready?" I ask.

"Ready," Nick says, and I hit the brakes so the back seat of the Camaro is lined up with the front seat of the van. Nick empties four rounds through the passenger window. The van skids and slides over into our lane, slamming into the car and pushing us off the road. I hear Nick's body slam into the roof of the car as we flip over.

8

BAD HISTORY

CHUNKS OF GLASS ARE STUCK TO MY FACE, MY PALMS. I CAN hear Nick's ragged breathing and the tinny, frantic voice of Mr. Z from the cellphone lying next to me. The Camaro is dead, not even the headlights are on. I want to say something, to ask Nick if he's okay, but I'm too afraid to speak. I'm still buckled in firmly, even though I'm upside-down. It feels like I may have broken a rib or three.

The van, it parked behind our car which came to a halt a hundred yards off the highway after flipping three times and knocking over some small trees. I hear a door open, close. I hear footsteps.

"Candy," Nick whispers. "Are you okay? You don't have to say anything. Just nod your head if you are." I move my head forward and back, as good as I can. "Okay," Nick says. "I've got him in my sights. When I start shooting, you run as far away as you can."

Run? I don't even know if I can move my legs. I nod anyway. The sound of someone approaching the vehicle grows louder. A shotgun cocks.

Chkchk.

I'm trying not to throw up as the blood gathers in my head.

"Come on out," the snake-like voice says. "You've got to pay for what you've done."

My hands are working furiously to release my seatbelt. My head feels tight with pressure, and my eyes feel like they'll burst. I'm afraid of falling on my head and breaking my neck, but if I stay here, I'm dead anyway.

"Hurry," Nick whispers.

Miraculously, I'm able to free myself and lower to the roof of the car. More glass bites into my skin causing cuts to bleed down my arms. Looking to my left, I can see the black polished shoes on the feet of the asshole with the shotgun. Pulling myself over to the passenger window, I see that the glass is gone, and I start to pull myself out. Then the shotgun blasts the seat I was just sitting in. Pellets spray all around, bits of glass hit my face, and I can't help but let out a scream. That is when Nick begins firing.

The next few moments seem to stretch out to days. What happens is I run as fast as I can and try to hide behind a nearby tree. As I'm running, I'm wondering if I'm wearing a decent enough ghost outfit.

"Get her!" The man with the shotgun shouts, and two more gunmen emerge from the rear of the van wearing dead president's faces. I'm reaching instinctively in my waistband for my gun. It's gone. Probably it fell out while I was tumbling in the car like a turd in a toilet. Sprays of bullets slap the tree as I dive behind it. Nick is still shooting. I can tell because he's the only one with a pistol. The *pop pop pop* continues on until Nick runs out of bullets.

"Shit!" Shotgun man screams as he falls to the ground. "He got me in the shin! Goddamnit!" he yells.

"He's dry," dead president number one says, moving closer in my direction.

"Let us take care of this bitch, and we'll handle him, too," dead president number two says. "Wouldn't be the first time you couldn't get it done," he says.

I'd tell you which president was which and all that, but honestly, I don't know my history all that well, and I'm kind of afraid I'm about to die, so the details are a little hazy.

Shotgun man moans on the ground, mumbles something which sounds like either 'fuck you,' or 'achoo.'

"Fuck your mother," dead president number one says. He's very close now. I can hear the crunch of leaves from just around the other side of the tree. If I run, I die. If I stay here, I die.

I hear shotgun man scream "Shit!" before a solitary *pop*. It seems Nick has found my pistol.

"Hey!" Dead president number two says. "You okay?"

Shotgun man is not okay.

—

"Go check on him!" Dead president one says to number two. "And you get the bitch," he says.

It doesn't take a genius to know that I'm the bitch. In a panic, I reach down, feeling for anything useful at all. Amazingly, I find something. Dead president number two comes around the tree and catches the sharp end of a heavy branch right between his stupid fucking dead president eyes. He goes down with a thud, blood trickling from the hole in his mask. I reach down, grab the sub-machine gun, and run and duck behind another tree, closer to the car and Nick.

"Harry?" Dead president number one says. "Did you get her?"

Harry isn't responding. If I didn't kill him, I came close.

"Harry?" he says again.

"Harry is unavailable at the moment!" I yell. I don't know exactly what possessed me to do this. I imagine Nick is still pinned under the car, and dead president number one was moments away from killing him. So maybe that's it. Maybe I don't want Nick to die.

Maybe I just don't want to be alone.

For a moment, I can't hear any movement.

"Damn you, you stupid bitch," the man says, finally.

Call it bravery, call it stupidity, but I come from behind the tree with the sub-machine gun pointed at dead president number one. He's only about ten feet away now, also pointing his gun at me.

"I hope you understand," he says. "That you're about to die. And you know why."

"Sorry," I say. "I can't say I do."

He laughs. "Sure you do." He tries to read my face. I'm hoping I can distract him long enough for Nick to take him down. He says, "Don't you? Surely they told you."

"Told me what?" I ask.

Before he can answer, the *whoop whoop* of a police siren accompanies red and blue flashing lights. It looks like someone reported the crash. The police car comes down the slope where the skid marks come off the highway. Out of the corner of my eye, I see Nick standing next to the car. He's motioning for me to run the other way.

I'm too scared to move. Frozen in place, I watch the

masked man in front of me turn to eye the police car. Dead president number one pulls his gun up, aims at the pair of policemen getting out of their car.

He begins firing.

9

THE MEXICAN

YOU'D BE RIGHT TO ASSUME THAT I WAS NEVER THE STAR OF the class known as 'physical education,' but you wouldn't know it if you saw me running through the woods, bullets snapping into trees and leaves all around me. Nick is maybe fifty yards to my left, doing the same. Neither of us have any idea where we're headed, just that there is a lot of shooting going on behind us.

Nick, he yells out something unintelligible. I turn and yell "What?!"

"Follow me!" He says.

And, what the hell, I do. The ground is getting soggy below my feet, and I know we've entered a swamp.

"Shh," Nick says. The shooting has stopped. We duck down behind a low bush, and he takes the sub-machine gun from me, cocking and reloading it.

I'm assuming that's what he's doing. I know shit-all about guns.

Nick motions for me to get down. I look up briefly and see a figure running toward our hiding spot. My heart is racing like a gerbil in a wheel as I stare at the soupy ground beneath us. Nick is crouched, gun pointed like a soldier in a bunker. His face shows no trace of fear or remorse. Maybe he's right. Maybe he *was* made for this. I know I wasn't.

You can blame this next part on me if you want to. I wouldn't agree with you, but maybe that's just my bias coming out. The figure running towards us, gun drawn, is getting much closer now. Me, I'm looking down, trying not to faint, so I can see what Nick can't. Swimming through the swampy water we're kneeling in, right next to Nick's leg, is the meanest looking snake I have ever seen. And like I said, blame me, forgive me, either way, I let out a little scream.

Please understand that it's not that I don't care what you think about me. I just can't waste time sugar-coating shit and selling it as candy (haha). Of course, Nick is startled by my audible ear-fucking, and he fires the gun. Well, let's just say this wouldn't be the first time Nick fucked up. The figure goes down, slumped against a tree. A pale sliver of moonlight coating his face and body is enough to tell me it was the cop that Nick shot. And just like that, it was just the two of us again.

The snake? It was scared away when I screamed. Which is a little bit funny when you think about it. That motherfucker grew legs. Neither Nick or myself has anything to say. After we exchange a look of *what the hell*, Nick reaches into his pocket and hands me the cellphone with Mr. Z on the other end. The call time is currently 21:13. I hold the phone up to my ear.

"Hello," is all I know to say.

"Are you both still alive?" The voice asks.

"Oh yeah," I say. "Never been more alive in my life. This is almost as exhilarating as Monster Truck Jam."

"We've pinged your location," Mr. Z says. "The Mexican

will be there to pick you up in seven minutes. He will take you to your next location. There will be a car waiting there."

"He better get here quicker than that," I say. "It's a shit-show out here."

"ETA is now six minutes, thirty-five seconds," Mr. Z says.

"Right," I say. "And this guy, The Mexican, how will we know him when we see him?"

Before hanging up, Mr. Z says, "He'll be Mexican."

—

Six minutes and thirty-five seconds later, an ice-cream truck pulls up with **NO WHEY JOSÉ** printed on the side. Out jumps a beefy man in a blue chambray work shirt and a cowboy hat. "You guys need ride?" he says.

"Yeah," Nick says. "We need."

"'Op in!" says The Mexican.

I move towards the truck and begin to open the passenger door. "Oh, no, no," The Mexican says. "Is no seat. Is only in back." He smiles, and I can see at least three silver teeth.

"Oh," I say. "That's *cool*." Nick chuckles.

I wasn't wrong. The back of that truck was colder than the old lady from the *Fox and the Hound*. You know, the scene where she drops Todd, the fox, off in the middle of the woods and just drives away? Right now, I almost feel as trau-matized as I did when I saw that scene as a child.

Nick and I slide onto the little bench in the back of the ice-cream truck. There are little cartons lying on the floor, puddles of melted ice-cream everywhere.

"We need get going!" hollers The Mexican through a little slit between the front and the back of the truck. "It's long way to Louisiana! I hope old Thelma can handle."

"Thelma?" Nick says.

"Yeah, man," The Mexican says, cranking the truck. "You're sittin' in her! She's all I got. But I figure, I've swum further, am I right?" he laughs.

I can't help but laugh, too. "How do you know Mr. Z?" I ask.

"I don't know what you're talking about, man," The Mexican says to me. Man, he says.

"Oh, right." I say. "Just a friendly lift across three states."

"That's right!" he yells over the roar of Thelma getting going. "Help yourselves to anything you wan' back there too, man. I got best vegan ice-cream in Leon County!"

"So, you're José then?" I ask.

"No way!" The Mexican says, and his laugh sounds like a dog choking on a bone.

Nick suggests we try to get some sleep, he reassures me that we probably won't die in these temperatures.

As I'm looking in the distance behind us, half a dozen police cars pull over in the spot we just left.

—

WHEN I OPEN my eyes again, it's bright outside. The truck has stopped. I look out the little slit of a window and see that we're at a gas station. The Mexican is nowhere around.

"Hey," I say, nudging Nick. "Get up."

Nick stirs, shivers, and sits up and looks at me. "Where

are we?" he asks.

"I don't know," I say. "But I'm getting right the fuck out of this truck, I know that."

Nick nods and goes to open the door. It's locked from the outside. "Why am I not surprised?" he says.

"I have to get out of here," I say. "I'm freezing, and I think I'm starting to go crazy." Truth is, I'd been feeling crazy for a long time.

After a few minutes, The Mexican returns to the truck. "Hey," he says. "I start to wonder if you two had actually die back there!"

"I'm going to die if I don't get out of here," I say.

"Can't do that," The Mexican grunts through the dividing window.

No way, José,

"So," Nick says. "Would you rather I take a dump in the Cherry Garcia, or the Rocky Road? Oh, I know. How about Monkey Madness?"

"You wouldn't," The Mexican says.

Nick begins to take off his belt.

—

NICK and I walk into the gas station and Arby's combo without saying a word. I need to figure out where we are, make sure we're headed in the right direction at least.

"Hi, welcome to Arby's," says an unfortunate creature with more teeth than mouth.

"Hi," I say. "Can you tell me where we are?"

"You're in Arby's, ma'am." she says. "Would you like to

try our six-piece jalapeño bites?"

My face flushes with anger, but only for a second. And then I ask, "Do those come in bigger sizes?"

—

Nick and I sneak into the family bathroom. Nick locks the door and moves his eyebrows up and down.

"Nope," I say.

"Okay," he says. "So, what do you think, should we just keep riding with this guy?"

"I think we're dead if we don't," I say.

"I found a brochure by the door," Nick says. "We're in Mobile, Alabama. Not too far now."

"And then we're on our own again," I say. "Okay, I guess we don't have a choice."

Someone knocks on the door.

"Hold your fucking horses, ese!" I yell.

I turn and look at Nick, he's got his pants on the floor, ass on the toilet. "Dude, are you serious?" I say.

"I wasn't playing about having to shit!" he says.

"But you couldn't wait for me to leave the room?" I ask.

"Sorry, I—" Nick begins but is cut off by a slamming fist on the door.

"Listen here, motherfucker!" I say, swinging the door open. It wasn't 'The Mexican' on the other side of the door. A horrified mother with a *can I speak to the manager* haircut is standing there, clutching her baby. She peers past me and sees Nick, naked from the waist down and pushing hard. He gives her a small wave.

10

SOMETHING FRUITY

I WISH I COULD TELL YOU THAT NICK AND I CAME UP WITH some grand escape plan, but ultimately, we weren't even sure we were in any danger with The Mexican. Except, of course, from freezing to death. After the fiasco in the shitter, Nick and I high-tail it back to the ice cream truck. The manager had been spoken to and was currently following behind us to make sure we left without any trouble.

"You done playing with your dick?" The Mexican says, leaning against the side of the truck.

"I guess," Nick says. "Let's just get going."

"I almost got into a fight with a soccer-mom, and Nick accidentally flashed his lil' weenie at her," I say. The Mexican laughs, spit flying from his mouth.

"Hey!" Nick says.

I wink at him.

We load back into the truck and hit the road.

—

IF ANYONE ever told you that New Orleans was anything but an enormous piece of shit, they lied to you. I hate this place as soon as The Mexican opens the back doors to let us out. The air smells like farts, there are potholes everywhere you look, and across the hotel parking lot, a car is being broken in to in the middle of the day.

"I can't wait to kill whichever sick fuck lives here," Nick says.

The Mexican stands there for a moment looking up at the fancy hotel, scratching his ass. "So, this is what is like, work for big boss?" he says.

"Trust me," I say. "We're not working for *big boss* by choice."

"You have choice," he says. He opens the driver door and gives a wave. "Good luck," he says and shuts the door.

Heather Wolworth and Benjamin Clancy check into the Garden Heights Hotel and Casino. This time, it's hard to keep up the rich girl persona. Forgive me, but I've just spent I don't know how many hours riding in a frozen box. And before that, I was knee-deep in swamp water. And let's not forget the major car accident I was in. I probably look like I just left a casting call for *Mad Max.*

When we arrive to our suite, there is once again a box on the bed. It has clothes, more weapons, more folders.

"You can read over that," I say to Nick, pointing at the folder. "I'm not doing anything until I shower and get some clean clothes on."

It isn't very long after I slip into the shower before Nick bangs on the door. "Candy!" He says. "Oh my God, Candy. This is crazy."

"What is it?" I ask, annoyed. This is my first time away from Nick in a long time, and I can't even enjoy it.

From the other side of the door, I hear Nick sigh. "The door is locked," he says.

"Is it?" I ask. But I knew. "Well, can it wait?" I say, my voice echoing in the hollow steamy box.

There's a few moments of silence from the other side of the door, and then Nick answers. "Yeah," he says. "It can wait. But it's so *cool.*"

When I finish in the bathroom, Nick is sitting on the bed. He's jittery with excitement. "Okay, Candy," he says. "Are you ready to hear who our next target is? Do you want to guess?"

"Oh, I know! Fred Flintstone," I say.

"Come on," Nick says. "Actually guess."

"I don't know, Nick."

"The biggest of the heavy hitters. You know, like on the podcast?" Nick says. "The Milwaukee cannibal?"

"Jeffrey Dahmer?" I ask.

"Jeffrey Dahmer," Nick says. "The people nommer."

"You mean his clone," I say. "We're supposed to kill his clone."

"Yeah," Nick says. "He works in the casino in this very hotel. Goes by the name of Steve Hicks." Nick hands me the folder with the information. The photograph paper-clipped to the inside of the folder shows a man in his late thirties. Any resemblance he has to the actual Jeffrey Dahmer eludes me.

"This doesn't make sense," I say. "Dahmer was caught in the nineties. This guy looks much older than that."

"What's your point?" Nick says.

"My point," I say, "is that they would have to have cloned him before he was even caught for him to be this old."

Nick thinks for a moment. "Well, we don't know how it works, do we?" He says.

"No," I say. "We sure don't. But I don't like this. I want to go home. I can't believe I let you get me into all of this."

"Well you're in it now," Nick says. "And tonight, we take care of our second target. The folder says we'll get double money this time. Maybe we're almost done, and we can move on with our lives. But right now, they've got us by the balls." He looks at me and chuckles. "Metaphorically, in your case," he adds.

—

In the evening Nick and I dress in the fancy clothes that were left by our 'employers.' We were given some cash for the casino. I've got a cream-colored cocktail dress. Nick is wearing a brand-new suit.

"Do you think we should split up?" Nick suggests.

"It could be dangerous," I say. But I see what Nick is saying. If this is the clone of Dahmer, he'll be a sexual being. Getting him alone will be much easier if we're not seen as a couple.

We enter the casino lobby around eight o'clock. "I'll find him," Nick says. "If he's Dahmer's clone, he'll most likely be into men. Just keep me in your sights. I'll text you." And then Nick disappears into the crowd.

Across the room is a bar with flashing lights and a super-cute bartender. "What can I get you?" He says as I take a seat.

"I don't know," I say. "Something fruity."

The bartender winks. "Coming right up, sweetie," he says, his voice flamboyant.

I glance around the room, looking for Nick. Finally, I spot him at a card table in the center of the room.

"This one is my specialty," the bartender says. "You're going to love it."

I take a sip of the pink drink. It's delicious but *strong*. My whole body shudders. "Damn," I say. "What's in this?"

"I never give away my secrets," the bartender says. "Is it good?"

"Very," I say.

"So," he says. "You here by yourself? No boyfriend?" he smiles. "No girlfriend?"

"Why?" I ask, sipping from my drink. "You know of any cute guys around here?"

The bartender chuckles. "Sorry, honey," he says. "No straight ones."

"Figures," I say.

"Oh, you're cute as a button," he says. "I wouldn't worry about finding someone."

"Thank you," I say, looking down at my drink. It's gone.

"Let me get you another," he says, eyeing my glass. "On me."

As the bartender makes me a new drink, I hear my phone ding.

The text from Nick reads: I think I found him. Not into guys. Come over here.

I look down and realize I'm halfway through my second drink, only I don't remember the bartender giving it to me. I try to stand up but my legs don't want to cooperate.

"*Whatdyouputinthere?*" I stammer.

"You okay there, hun?" The bartender says, his voice

warping inside my head. I'm trying not to puke as I pull the text messenger app up on my phone and manage to text Nick: Help.

11

PARTY TRICK

I AWAKE IN TOTAL DARKNESS WONDERING WHAT THE HELL happened. The room I'm in is cold and silent, save for a *swish-swish* sound every twenty seconds or so. My arms are bound behind my back with some sort of cloth. There is a blindfold covering my eyes. I want to scream out, call for Nick, for anyone at all, to help me. Chuck Norris please, or The Rock. Hell, at this point I'd take Steve Urkel riding a purple giraffe.

But no one comes.

And then a female voice from across the room says, "Do you want to see a trick?"

I scream, but it would be more accurate to say that I bark like a yorkie at the pizza man. Chill bumps go down my arms as I think about how close my captor is.

"A trick?" I say. "Yeah. Show me how fast you can get these ropes off of me. That'd be a trick."

"I'm trying to be nice," the voice says. "I'm not the mean one. It's just you and me."

"Oh yeah?" I say, my face half buried in what feels like a

pillow. "The mean one, then? Where is the mean one? Out knocking over mailboxes?"

"Something like that," the voice says. "Anyway, you can call me Christina."

"You can call me Shirley," I say.

"But your name is Candy," Christina says. "Is Shirley your middle name?"

"Never mind," I say. "Can you let me out of this? Tell me what's going on?"

"I can't let you out," she says. "But I can take your blindfold off, if you want to see my trick. Do you want to see my trick?" Another *swish-swish.*

"Sure," I say. Whatever the fuck it takes.

Footsteps rattle across the room as Christina approaches. "Don't do anything crazy, okay?" She says. "I mean it, this isn't a movie. If you fuck with me, I'll put a bullet in your skull."

Whoa there, Christina, if you're the nice one I'd hate to meet the mean one. Which I will, of course.

"I'm not going to do anything," I say.

"Good," she says. Then the world gets a lot brighter as I find myself in a hotel room just like mine, only mirrored. One of the corner rooms.

Standing in front of me is a short, mousy blonde girl in a purple skirt and a white blouse. Christina looks like she escaped from a schoolgirl magazine photo shoot.

"Hi there," she says with a wave.

"Can you help me to sit up?" I ask.

"No can do, missy," Christina says. "Sean wouldn't have it. In fact, if he sees I took off your blindfold, he won't be happy about that, either. But it's okay. I can just tell him you slipped it off by rubbing your face against the bed. And you'll agree, won't you?"

I don't say anything.

Christina turns around, opens a drawer. Pointing a pistol at my forehead, she says, "WON'T YOU?"

"Yeah," I say. "Sure, whatever. Damn."

Christina's face brightens. "Thanks!" She says in a bubbly, girlish outburst. She puts the gun down on the nightstand. "Now, check this out," she says. She holds up a small, circular object.

"What is it?" I say.

Christina moves closer. In her hand is a red yo-yo. Printed on the side of the yo-yo is a white thumb.

"Oh," I say. "A yo-yo. Yo-yo tricks. Neat."

"You're damn right it's neat," Christina says. "I've got tricks that would blow your mind. Takes a lot of practice, but I find it to be therapeutic. And I'm not talking about the sleeper, either. I'm talking about some real razzle dazzle shit."

I have no idea what she's rambling about, but it seems to keep her calm. Until I think of some way out of this, I have to indulge her.

"That is pretty cool, actually." I say. "And what's the significance of the thumb?"

Christina smiles. "Let me show you a real trick first," she says.

Slowly the yo-yo descends to the floor and returns to Christina's hand. "Watch this," she says. She swings her arm around wildly, letting the yo-yo go like a fastball.

Next to the bed, the yo-yo knocks the lime wedge from the corner of a glass into some greenish liquid. The lime wedge splits in two. Christina retracts the yo-yo into a gloved hand.

"The trick," Christina says, "is that I've added tiny razor blades to the edges of the yo-yo. It's been a lot of fun learning new tricks, but it's incredibly hard to get blood out of string. I have to take a spool of yo-yo string with me everywhere I go!"

"That sounds...inconvenient," I say, squinting at the yo-yo. And there they were. Around the edges of the red plastic were tiny embedded razors.

"Do you want to hear a secret?" Christina asks.

"Um. Of course I do," I say.

"Truth is," she says, "I refuse to fire a gun. That's why I modified this guy," she says, holding out the yo-yo. "Sean pretends it doesn't bother him, but I know it does."

"You wanna see another trick?" She says, bobbing the toy up and down.

"Can you tell me what is going on here?" I say. "Please?"

"Girl, calm the fuck down." She says. "Let me show you my trick, and then we can talk."

I lay quietly, waiting for this big trick. Christina fumbles through drawers. She comes out with a small, orange ping-pong ball.

"Now," she says. "You can't move for this trick. Okay? I mean it. It could be really bad if you move even a hair."

"What are you going to do?" I ask, my voice shaky.

"You'll see," she says with a wink. "Okay, the moving stops now." She tilts my head back, places the orange ball in my ocular socket, resting on my eyeball.

"Don't do this," I say.

"Stop moving!" Christina shouts. She jerks my head back and re-adjusts the ball. "There," she says. "Just like that."

I can feel hot tears rolling down my face. I close my eyes and pray for Steve Urkel to come through the door with a machine gun. A cigar hanging from the corner of his mouth.

Swish-swish.

"Fore!" Christina exclaims.

Instinctively, I jerk back. I watch as the red yo-yo explodes the ping-pong ball like the peaceful planet of Alderaan. I watch as the yo-yo smashes into the bridge of my nose and gives me a huge white 'thumbs-up.' And once again, Christina has ruined her white string.

"Goddamnit!" Christina says. "You fucking moved!"

Blood is pouring out of the side of my nose; the smell is powerful. "I'm so fucking sorry," I say. "I hate to ruin your party trick!"

"Whoa, whoa," says another voice. A door shuts and in walks the man known as Sean. Sean is the bartender who was slipping me drinks. The ones that got me in this predicament.

"Motherfucker," I say.

"Hey, sweetie," he says. "You were so thirsty this evening!" He looks at my nose. "Oh no, did Christina show you her stupid yo-yo tricks?" He laughs. "Well damn, Christina, get some rags or something!"

Christina walks into the bathroom.

Sean smiles down at me. "Kind of awkward," he says.

"What's that?" I say.

"Well, it's just—you know—I have this whole speech to give," he says. "And I have to wait on Christina to come back with some toilet paper or whatever. So you don't die of blood loss. We need you alive for the final trick. So, you see what I mean. Awkward."

"What a shame," I sneer.

Christina returns to the room with gobs of paper towels. She presses some to my face.

"Where is Nick?" I ask. "I know you know who I'm talking about."

Sean and Christina laugh.

"He's closer than you think," Sean says. "What do you say, Christina? Untie her?"

"Sure," Christina says. "You got your gun?"

"Oh, I'm not worried about that," Sean says. "Candy will behave."

Christina rolls the yo-yo up and down, up and down.

Swish-swish. Swish-swish.

She reaches behind me with the toy in her hand. I feel a tugging, and my wrists are free. She does the same with my ankles, cutting with the edge of the yo-yo.

I roll to a more comfortable position on my back, and almost fall off the bed when I see Nick lying next to me, unconscious.

Sean walks around to Nick's side of the bed, splashes the greenish drink with the limes in his face.

"*Whatafuck?*" Nick says, bolting upright. He glances around the room, sees Christina. "You," he says. "You bitch. Is this your trick? What did you do? Drug me?"

"I was just telling your friend Candy about my yo-yo," Christina replies, ignoring Nick's insult. "You see what happened to her face? That was a bit of a...mishap. But it can be worse, if my last trick doesn't go in your favor."

Sean pulls up a chair, aims the gun he wasn't worried about.

"Now that I have your attention," Christina continues, "let me explain the rules of my last trick to you. Do you see the thumb on the side?" She asks.

"Yeah," Nick says. He spits in her direction. Sean stands up.

"If you do something like that again," Sean says, "this party will be over a lot sooner than you were hoping."

"As I was saying," Christina says, "this yo-yo has razors in it. It spins at over ten-thousand rotations per minute. It will take your head clean off your body in one swipe. But, depending on how you play the game, it could be your lucky day."

"I feel so special," I say.

"For my last trick, I'm going to let the yo-yo fall." Christina says.

"That's it?" Nick says.

"No. That's not it," Christina says. "See, the little white thumb determines your fate. We can use the standard sex symbols. If the yo-yo stops with the thumb up, Nick dies. If it stops with the thumb down, Candy dies. That's all there is to it."

My stomach has turned. I'm swaying from side to side, heart beating hard.

"Are you ready for my trick?" Christina asks.

Nick and I exchange a look. Neither of us speak. Sean's pistol pointed at our faces isn't helping.

"Okay, here we go!" She says, giggling.

Swish-swish. The yo-yo goes down a final time.

The ragged spinning of the white thumb rotating on our death-wheel is driving me mad. What drives me more mad is the fact that I want the thumb to just point down. Just let it be me. I'm tired of tricks.

Before I even realize what's happened, the yo-yo has stopped. I don't want to look. I don't think I can.

"Nick," Sean says. "It's a big ole 'thumbs-up!'"

"No," Nick says. "This isn't fair. What do you want from us? Just tell us!"

Christina winds the yo-yo up. "Say goodbye, Nick," she says.

Nick is crying next to me. This time, I don't blame him.

"Wait," Sean says. "Oh my gosh, hold the phone! We almost forgot the rule to this trick! Didn't we, Christina?!"

"Oh my," she exclaims. "You're right!"

"What are you talking about?" I say.

"The rule for this trick," Christina says, "is this: if the thumb works against your favor, you have a choice."

"What choice?" Nick asks.

"You can accept your fate," Christina says. "Or you can let it be her," she says, pointing to me.

"But if it's her," Sean says. "Then you have to kill her."

12

TROJAN HORSE

THE WALLS OF THIS CORNER HOTEL ROOM ARE CLOSING IN. Nick has to choose who dies—himself or me—and I have a feeling I know what he's going to do. But then, of course, I have to ask myself what I would do given the same choice. Again, I feel that sickening feeling of *just let it be me*. I mean, I've been gone all this time, and my mom hasn't even called to bitch about me being gone. Okay, okay, that's not fair. I had a good cover story. I guess I just want to be missed. To be loved.

"Nicholas?" Sean says. "Time to choose, pal. Who dies? You or her?" He points at me. The *swish-swish* of the yo-yo is digging into my brain.

If looks could kill, I'd be a murderer. Which, I'd like to remind you, I'm still not.

Nick opens his mouth to speak, closes it.

Swish-swish.

"You've got about ten seconds to decide," Christina says. "Or I'll just kill both of you."

"I..." Nick says.

"Ten," Sean says.

"Damn!" Christina exclaims. "I'd sure hate to be you."

"Seven," Sean continues.

A phone begins ringing in the room. The standard iPhone chime.

"Damnit," Sean says, checking the screen of his phone. "It's the boss."

"Answer it," Christina says.

Sean sighs. Walks into the bathroom. Christina shifts her gaze in my direction. "You shouldn't have come here," she says. "We told you people to stay out of our way."

"I have no fucking clue what you're talking about," I say. "Honestly."

From the bathroom I can hear Sean saying, "Where?" saying, "Right now?" There is fear in his voice.

"What is it?" Christina shouts.

"They're coming," Sean says in a frantic voice. "Four black vans parked out front." He shoots a glance in our direction. "I'm sorry," he says. "This is a big misunderstanding. But we could use your help, if you want to stay alive."

Nick, wiping sweat from his forehead, he says, "A big misunderstanding? A big misunderstanding is your wife thinking you were cheating on her with your lesbian secretary. This isn't that. This is me dying."

And there it is. Him, dying. Not me.

"We can talk about this later," Sean says, freeing Nick's bindings. "Right now, we have a problem we need your help with."

"Why would we help you?" I ask.

"Because," Christina says, freeing my wrists. "If you don't, we might *all* die."

"What are you talking about?" I say. And then I remember. Black vans. Could it be the people who followed Nick and I when we left Tallahassee?

"Just—" Sean says, but is cut off when a fist slams against the door.

Bam bam bam.

Sean holds a finger to his mouth, opens a suitcase, hands me a pistol. Hands one to Nick.

"We need to get out of here," Christina whispers.

"The balcony," I whisper. "It's the only way."

"It isn't," Sean whispers. "Our room is connected to yours. We can get the drop on them."

"What do they want?" Nick whispers.

"They want us dead," Sean replies.

—

WE MAKE it through the doors between the rooms and get the door shut just quick enough to miss the shotgun blast that decimates the door of Christina and Sean's room. We lock the door behind us, and, frantic, I grab my things off the bed.

"Here's what we do," Sean says. "They're expecting us. Not you guys. So, I'll pop into the hallway, start some fire that way. Get them to follow me into this room, while you two go behind them and take them out from behind. They won't see it coming."

"They may be expecting us," I say. "We've...dealt with them before. Whoever they are."

"It's all we have," Sean says. And we're not given any time to think about it. Sean bursts into the hallway and starts shooting like Neo in *The Matrix*. I can neither confirm nor deny whether he turns in a slow-motion circle.

What happens next is important, so pay attention. Nick pulls me close as the gunfire echoes down the hall. He puts his lips on mine and kisses me like a horny adolescent making out with his pillow. The kiss seems to drag forever, and when he's done kissing me, he shoves me into the space between the rooms, locking the door. I'm stuck—safe— between the two rooms.

"Damnit!" I yell, blood flushing my face. "Let me out!" He can't do this alone. I don't know why I care, but he just can't.

I kick against the wood of the door. Nothing happens, except for a painful surge up my sciatic nerve. And then I remember the gun. I grit my teeth, turn my head, and fire at the handle. It takes three shots, the sound deafening in the enclosed space.

With a kick, the door is open. I can hear reports of gunfire from the hallway. I can see Nick standing in the doorway. Without a glance in my direction, he moves down the hall. I want to shout his name, to ask him to come back to me, but I can't—my throat won't make the sounds. I make my way to the doorway to follow Nick, when I see a monster of a man walk by. He's got a mask on his face, a massive knife in his right hand.

If you've been paying attention, you'll know that to this point, I haven't killed a soul. Not directly. And I didn't know if I ever could, until I was put in a situation where I had no choice. You don't get charged with murder if you retaliate against an assailant in your own home. Why should this be any different?

Down the hall, I watch the hulking figure grab Nick around the chest, holding the knife to his throat.

"I got him!" The man shouts. "The little fucker from the

IHOP!" The man begins to slowly draw the blade across Nick's neck. Blood spurts across the floor and walls.

"No!" I shout. My mistake. The guy drops Nick to the floor, turns on me. He runs at me with the bloody knife.

My hands are shaking like a crackhead writing a check. Nick, on the floor, he looks at me. *Do it*, his face says. *Fucking do it.*

I do it, and a bullet enters my attacker's brain like a Trojan horse.

13

119 SUNRISE DRIVE

As RANDOM HOTEL GUESTS BEGIN TO FILL THE HALLS, clutching their cellphones in their hands, calling the police, I'm holding my hand to Nick's throat in an attempt to stop the blood from shooting out in pints.

"They're all down," Sean says, panting. "It worked." He sees Nick lying on the floor, takes off his shirt, and rips a section of cloth free. "Take away your hand," he says to me. And when I do, I see that the cut isn't nearly as bad as it could be.

"I don't think he hit the jugular," Sean says, wrapping the cloth around Nick's neck. "No, I'm sure they didn't," he says. "You'll be okay."

Nick's face flashes a glimpse of relief. If I hadn't been looking at how much blood was on my hands, I probably wouldn't have noticed them shaking so badly.

Because, of course it had to be said, if only in my mind: Because I *killed* someone. And what was worse—I didn't feel bad about it.

Christina pops her head out of the room Nick and I had

planned to sleep in. "We need to go," she says. "Cops will be up here any minute."

"You're damn right they will!" Shouts an old man in a worn LSU Tigers bathrobe.

"Go back in your room, sir," Sean says.

"Fuck you!" Says the old man, holding his phone in front of him. "I'm filming this," he says. "It'll be on the news before—"

Sean draws his gun, points it at the man, and fires, western shootout style. The man screams as his cellphone explodes in his hand.

"Like I said," Sean says, "get your old ass back in your room before something bad happens to you." More onlookers down the hall retreat into their rooms, and the old man in the bathrobe decides he better do the same.

"We have to go!" Christina shouts.

"Help me get him up," Sean says, wrapping an arm around Nick.

"I'm fine," Nick says.

"You're anything but, my friend," Sean says.

"Oh," Nick says, "so we're friends now, are we?"

"We won't be anything if we keep standing here," I say. And then I see the police lights dancing on the walls, coming through the windows.

Red. White. Blue.

God. Bless. America.

And bless our boys in blue, right? But the boys in blue can't help us. They will take us to prison for the rest of our lives if they catch us. And I'm afraid I'm not quite ready to eat a bullet.

"Okay," I say, thinking, my voice shaking. "They'll probably take the elevator, right? Or would they take the stairs?"

"Stairs," Christina says. "That's what they do in movies. In case there's a bomb or something in the elevator."

"What the fuck are you talking about?" Sean blurts. "We have no idea which way they'll go."

"Here's what we do," Nick says, his voice ragged as he holds the blood-soaked cloth to his neck.

—

"OFFICERS! OFFICERS!" Sean calls. "They went that way! At least half a dozen of them. They shot my friend here," he points at Nick who raises his hand in a weak wave.

"Stay put," says the officer leading the group. He draws his weapon.

"They're hiding out in the last room on the right," Christina says. "Please, please catch them!"

The cops rush down the hall, enter the room on the end. Me, I press the elevator button. The officers shout commands to the empty rooms as we enter the elevator and press the button for the first floor.

—

THIRTY MINUTES LATER, and against my better judgement, Nick and I are in the back of Sean and Christina's SUV parked behind a long closed-down Feed and Seed plant.

Sean shuts off the engine and steps out of the vehicle. The rest of us follow suit.

"Let me see your neck," Christina says, grabbing Nick by the arm. Nick begins to unwind the bloodied shirt around his throat. "It's really not as bad as I thought it was," he says. "It's already clotted up."

Christina pulls a flashlight from her purse, clicks it on, and holds it up with her gloved hand. It's pretty nasty, but Nick's right. It's dried. He's very lucky.

"Tell me what the hell is going on," I say. "Who did you think we were?"

Sean pulls a pack of cigarettes out of his pocket and offers me one. I take it.

Nick says, "I'd take one but I'd have smoke coming out of my throat like a blowhole."

As Sean lights my cigarette, Nick flashes a jealous glance.

"Well," Sean says, "we assumed you were with *them*. You know, the black-van people. The ones who are trying to stop us from accomplishing our mission."

"And what is your...mission?" Nick asks. As I'm staring at the stars, buzzing from the cigarette, I can't imagine what Sean's answer will be. I can't imagine it making any sense.

Christina fidgets uncomfortably. "Sean..."

Sean and Christina share a glance, their eyes doing the talking. "Why don't you guys tell us what you were doing at the hotel?" Sean says.

"I asked first," I say.

"I don't really give a shit," Sean says, changing the mood.

"Whoa now," Nick says. "Just what the hell—"

"Look," Sean says, taking a drag from his cigarette. "It's like this: I'm not going to answer you unless you answer me first. If you don't want to answer, that's fine. But I won't either."

"We were sent here to kill Jeffrey Dahmer," Nick blurts.

Once again, if looks could kill, I'd be a murderer.

Sean laughs. "Dahmer? Dahmer is six feet deep and full of worm shit!"

"It's his clone," Nick says.

"Nick," I say. "Maybe you need to sit down, seems you're a bit lightheaded."

"I'm fine. And I'm done with fake names and bullshit like that. The man asked what we came to do, and I'm telling him," Nick says.

Christina rifles through her purse, pulls out a crumpled-up flier and shows it to me. "Is this the guy?" She asks.

It's our guy. And there's some writing at the bottom of the picture.

Known N.W.O. Figure. Cult leader. Dangerous.

My gaze shifts between the man in the photograph and Sean's face, reading his expression. He's completely serious.

"Who gave you this?" I say. "Who are you working for?"

"To be honest," Christina says, "we don't know who they are. Just that they have some pretty incriminating stuff on us. This was the only way out of it. We're taking out these New World Order cult guys. If we do what they say, we're free to go. At least at some point, I hope so."

"At least the guys we're taking down are scum." Sean says. "But what was that about Jeffrey Dahmer? Were you serious?"

"We were told we were hunting the clones of serial killers..." Nick says. He looks defeated, sad. "I don't know what to think anymore."

"We've been lied to," I say. "Either we have, or you guys

have, or we both have. We need to find out the truth. Who are these people we're killing?"

"We have Mr. Hicks' address," Christina says. "We could go see him. Find out what we can."

I look at Nick, who shrugs. "I guess we might as well," he says.

"I'll drive," Sean says.

—

"119 SUNRISE DRIVE," Sean says, putting the vehicle in park. He reaches into the glovebox, puts his pistol in his waistband. "Just in case," he says.

We walk up the driveway. It's late. Really late. I'm wondering if Steve Hicks will even answer his door. Is he still at work?

Nick rings the doorbell. A few moments pass by. Finally, I hear a voice say, "Who is it? At this time of night? Someone better be dead!"

Plenty of people are dead.

"Mr. Hicks," Sean says through the closed door. "We just have a few questions for you."

"Go away," the man says from inside the house. "Whatever you're selling, I ain't buying."

"We're not trying to sell you anything, sir," Christina says. "We're trying to potentially save your life."

A pause. A chain sliding.

The door cracks open a few inches. "Are you from ViaLab?"

"We're not," I say, making a mental note to remember that name. "But could we come in? We need to talk."

Steve Hicks sticks his head out of the door, taking nervous glances around his front yard. "Sure," he says. "Come in."

We are seated around the dinner table, waiting in silence as Steve Hicks makes coffee.

"So," Sean says. "Can you tell us why people would want you dead? I hate to jump straight to the nitty-gritty, but this is pretty serious."

"Want me dead?" Steve laughs from across the room, a jittery little noise. "Who *doesn't* want me dead?" He comes over to the table, a tray of mugs in his hands. As he passes them out, I can't help but think of IHOP. Dumb as it is, I could go for some IHOP.

"Who did that to you, son?" Steve asks Nick. "You're bloodied up pretty bad."

"It's a long story," Nick says.

"I've got time," Steve replies.

"It's not important," Nick says, taking a sip of his coffee. "What's important is what we came here for. We need to know why some people might want you dead."

"Where do I begin?" Steve says. Another nervous chuckle. "I guess it starts with ViaLab. Always ViaLab."

"What's ViaLab?" Christina asks.

Steve's hands shake as he stares into his coffee. He looks like he lost something in there.

"ViaLab," Steve says, "is—"

But Steve Hicks will never speak again, because as he takes his last sip of coffee, a tiny red dot hovers over the bottom of his mug. And before he can finish his sentence, half of his brain is painted across the walls behind his seat.

14

SPLITTING THE DIFFERENCE

FOR A GROUP OF PEOPLE WHO HAVE SEEN THEIR FAIR SHARE OF death, we don't handle this well. Steve Hicks—definitely NOT Jeffrey Dahmer—is slumped on the table with his thoughts spilling out everywhere. I hope you're not eating. I mean, I just can't get over how nasty this is, Steve's brain is everywhere, little shards of uncooked sausage. Some of it in my hair. Blood is caked on my face like a sneeze.

In a swift jerking motion, Sean is on his feet. "Come on!" He screams, peeking through the blinds. I can hear a vehicle's engine running outside.

The rest of us get to our feet. Sean is already out the front door, sprinting toward his SUV.

"What the hell are you doing?" Nick shouts.

Sean, opening the driver door, he says, "We have to follow them! Find out what they know."

It's a silver Toyota Camry that's bolting away from Steve Hick's house. Whoever is driving the thing definitely saw us leaving the house. We pile into Sean's SUV, and Sean backs out of the driveway.

"They just turned right at the end of the street!"

Christina shouts. She's clutching her yo-yo in one gloved hand like a security blanket.

"Why are we chasing them down?" I ask. "They're obviously dangerous!"

"So are we," Sean says, gripping a semi-automatic pump shotgun, nuzzled between the front two seats. "And we really need to find out what the hell is going on. These people could have been from—"

"ViaLab," I say. "I know..."

"Turn here!" Christina shouts from the passenger seat. Her demeanor has completely changed. No longer fidgeting with her yo-yo, now she's letting out a battle cry of sorts. "We can catch them!" She yells.

Sean presses the accelerator to the floor. The engine screams, and the car in front of us hits the brakes, turns a hard left. "Son of a bitch," Sean mutters, slowing the vehicle. We turn down the same street as the Camry, now only a few car-lengths behind.

"Umm..." Nick says, pointing. But I already see it. A few hundred yards ahead, a set of railroad tracks cross our street. Shooting from the left at a dangerous pace is a train.

"If they put that train between us, we'll never catch them," Sean says.

"There's no way," I say. "That thing is *moving*. It'll cross before they can."

The Camry slows for a half-second—I don't know if they were looking for another way to go, but it doesn't matter—it was enough. A half-second was the difference between life and death. After the quick hesitation, the Camry speeds up, heading straight for the tracks.

"They're crazy!" Nick yells.

Sean presses down on the brakes and the horn of the train bellows again. And again, once more, before tearing the silver Camry in half. The sound of it was like multiple buildings collapsing simultaneously. Metal against metal, screeching and glass breaking. The train didn't even slow, at least not at first. The train had clipped the Camry just in front of the driver door, but the force of it was enough to rip the vehicle in two, sending the halves flying backwards—the front half smashed through a stop sign, and the back half landed in a thrift store.

"Hurry!" Sean says, getting out of the SUV. "Let's check it out before the cops come."

The back half of the car is closest to us, and we step through the broken storefront and check out the damage. The backseat of the car is splattered with blood and various body parts.

"I'm going to be sick," Nick says.

"Me too," I agree.

"There's nothing of importance that I can see," Christina says, letting the yo-yo *swish-swish.*

"Let's go check the front," Sean says. He climbs through the windows and rushes across the street. The rest of us follow behind him with a lot less enthusiasm. I've seen enough dead people to last me until the end of time. Unfortunately, I'll see a lot more before this is over.

"Holy shit," Sean says. "It's really fucking bad."

He's right. There are two bodies. Well, at least I assume there *were* two bodies. I only see two heads. The bodies are mashed together into a pulpy mess straight out of a cheesy 80's horror flick. The train is almost to a complete stop now.

"Look!" Christina says. She grabs a notebook that was lying on the ground next to the front half of the car. She shoves the papers back into it and sticks it under her arm. "Okay," she says. "Let's get out of here."

—

"WE HAVE to get out of town," Sean says. "We'll find somewhere to stop and rest. Just not here."

We all agree with Sean. Nick and I are sitting in the backseat while Sean drives and Christina thumbs through the notebook. "Well, they weren't from ViaLab, that's for sure," she says. She passes the notebook into the backseat. Nick takes it, opens to the first page, and holds it open so I can see.

There's a photo of Steve Hicks but the name is different.

Rahkim Mohamed Abdullah. He is one of the men responsible for multiple acts of terrorism on U.S. Soil. American alias unknown.

"What the fuck?" Nick says. "He doesn't even look like... well, you know."

"A lot of people convert to Islam, change their names," Sean says from the front. "But that's not what's happening here. This is bigger than we realized."

Christina moans. "I want this to be over," she says.

"I have an idea," I say. "We need to find somewhere safe to stop though."

Sean nods. We drive on for a few more miles, until we find an exit with FOOD on the sign.

"Who's hungry?" Sean asks.

—

WE FIND a small quiet diner in a town called Brookhaven. The jukebox is playing country music at a respectable volume, and there's only seven people in the whole building, including the four of us. I'm carrying the notebook under one arm.

A waitress named Cori tells us to feel free to sit wherever we like. We cram into a small booth in the back corner of the diner.

"So, what do we know so far?" Sean says.

"We know that three different groups of people were given three different descriptions of the same man," Nick says. "And told to kill him."

"Which," I say, "would indicate that we're all somehow working for the same people, more or less."

"At the very least, people with the same motives," Christina says.

Cori comes, takes our orders, and bounces away, ass shaking. Nick stares.

I clear my throat. "Well," I say. "My idea is this: we have to call and tell our contact when we...finish a job, right?"

"Right," the other three say in unison.

"So," I continue, "you guys call your contact, claim the job. Then we'll call ours, and see what happens if we claim it, too."

"What is that going to prove?" Christina asks.

"It may not prove anything," I say, "but it could prove that they're connected. I don't know."

"But we're not killing any more of the targets?" Christina asks.

"I don't think so," I say. "But I want to find out what's going on. What's ViaLab? I have so many questions."

"Well," Nick says. "Who is your contact?"

"Oh," Sean says. "You mean Mr. Z?"

15

IN BLOOM

Since this is my story, I guess it makes sense that everyone looks to me every time we have no idea what to do next. It doesn't make it any easier.

"Well," Christina says, "this is interesting."

"The thing is," Nick says, "those other people, the ones who got creamed by that train, they probably worked for Mr. Z, too. And he probably knows they're dead."

Sean stirs a spoon in his coffee cup. Small white particles float in concentric circles. "All we can do is call him," he says.

"Okay," I say, "but who calls? Us, or you guys? Also, what do we say?"

"I'll do it," Nick says. He pulls his phone out of his pocket. I should have stopped him. I should have realized Nick couldn't handle it, but it doesn't matter anymore.

Nick finds Mr. Z in his phone and presses send. The waitress—Cori—comes to the table, and Sean waves her away.

Nick presses the speaker button on his phone, looks over

his shoulder—there's no one in earshot—and sets his phone on the table.

"Yes?" Mr. Z says.

"It's done," Nick says.

"What's done?" Mr. Z says, sounding annoyed.

"You know," Nick says, "Steve- er, Dahmer. We took care of him."

There is a pause on the line. Nick looks around the table in apprehension.

"Tell me," Mr. Z says, "why are you lying to me, Nick?"

Nick swallows. "Um," he says, "what do you mean?"

"Sean," Mr. Z says.

Silence.

"Sean, I know you're there, damnit." Mr. Z says.

"Yeah," Sean says, "I'm here."

"This experiment has been terminated," Mr. Z says. "Do not look for us. We have locked your accounts, all four of you. I do not know how this happened, and I don't care, but you no longer work for us."

The call ends.

"They're tracking these goddamn phones," Sean says. "I guarantee it."

"Shit!" I say. "Shit! Shit! Shit!"

"What do we do?" Christina wails.

Nick pulls back the curtains, squints outside. He's mumbling to himself.

"If they've been following our locations on the phones, they could be right on top of us," Sean says.

"Go!" Nick says, shoving me out of the seat, my ass crashing onto the floor.

"Hey!" I say, "what the hell?!"

"Go! Go! Go!" Nick says. The waitress is walking towards us again. "Get down!" Nick shouts.

The poor girl just stands there, staring. I don't know which breaks first, the coffee pot she drops, or the window behind us, but Cori's body is riddled with gunfire, her white apron exploding like a rose in bloom. Tiny shards of glass mist the back of my neck as burst gunfire rains down on the diner. I've got cuts up and down my palms from crawling on the glass-littered floor. Christina is ahead of me, making her way towards the kitchen door on her hands and knees.

"Shit!" Nick shouts. I turn and see he's got a massive chunk of glass in his shoulder. He sees me slowing, yells, "keep going!" And I hurry, following Christina around through the flapping kitchen door.

Another shattering sound and then a hissing sound. The restaurant is filling with smoke at an alarming rate. But just before the cloud fills the place, I spot Sean, still sitting in the booth, splayed out like a drunk in an alley. Chunks of his face and scalp are missing. He's a puzzle that will never be complete again. I'm wondering if Christina knows. Probably not—not yet. I turn around and enter the kitchen. A huge man in a chef's apron is facing me, holding a shotgun. I throw my hands into the air.

"Is it the Russians?" He barks. "Or the Koreans?"

"I don't know!" I say.

"Get behind me!" He yells. Nick, Christina, and I go past the cook, and head for the back door.

"Where is Sean?" Christina cries.

"Come on," I say, gripping her by the shoulder. "We can probably get to the car while this guy plays the hero."

The back door is so close. If only Christina would cooperate.

"I can't leave him like this!" She says.

"You can't take him like this either!" Nick says, turning her to face her. "Do you understand? He's gone. If you don't come with us, you'll be gone too. But if you come with us, you'll have a chance for revenge. We're going to get these fuckers. Aren't we, Candy?"

Christina turns to look at me, tears streaming down her face. And although I hadn't thought about our next course of action, I knew. I had to know what was going on. I couldn't let these people continue doing what they were doing, knowing what I knew. I also had a sneaking suspicion that they would never stop hunting us. That they would never let us live.

"I..." I stutter. "What choice do we have?"

Christina looks unconvinced, I need to motivate her further. "Christina," I say, "we're going to get them back. All of them. Now come with us." I reach out my hand, and Christina takes it in her own.

The sound of gunfire is getting closer. The cook, whose name I never learned, is standing in the doorway to the kitchen firing one shotgun shell after another, letting out a primal scream. Nick pulls his pistol from his waistband and kicks open the back door. After sticking his head outside, he looks back at me and motions for us to follow. Pulling Christina behind me, the three of us make it out of the diner alive.

—

OUTSIDE THE DINER, I can hear boots stomping the asphalt as more bodies enter the front of the building. The SUV is parked out front.

"Okay," I whisper. "We're going to have to run for it. They

should all be inside by the time we make it to the front of the building. We'll need the keys ready. Where are they?"

Christina, who is in rough shape already, goes as rigid as a surfboard.

"Sean had them," Nick says for her.

"Do either of you know how to hot-wire a vehicle?" Christina asks. I guess that isn't *that* crazy of a question, considering everything else we've seen and done, but no, Nick and I are not spies from a James Bond film.

"Sorry," I say, "sure don't."

The gunfire inside has ceased, shotgun blasts included.

"They have Hummers parked on the other side of the building," Nick says. "I saw them getting out before the shooting started. There's at least four of them."

"They probably have tracking devices on those too!" Christina nearly shouts.

"Yeah," I say, "you're right. But it will get us out of here. Let's try it."

Not one, but *all* of the vehicles were left running, keys in the ignition. I open the driver door of the Hummer closest to us, Nick gets in the passenger seat, and Christina sits behind me. I'm struggling to move the seat forward when the first bullet smacks into the windshield right in front of Nick's face. I'm not one-hundred-percent sure, but I believe Nick shit himself. Of course, the glass is tempered with something. The bullet went through the outermost layer, sticking in place in the reinforced glass. Small veins of cracked glass spider away from the bullet-hole.

I get the seat adjusted so my foot can actually touch the pedal and slam it to the floor. The Hummer lurches forward like an ornery bull. After knocking down a sign and catching a few more bullets, we're gone.

"Is everyone okay?" I ask. I'm immediately sorry for

saying it. *Everyone* is clearly not okay. Sean has cashed in his chips. Game over. "Christina," I say, "I'm sorry. That was a dumb question."

"No, it's fine," she says. Her voice is small and sad. I decide to drop it.

I'm driving, and I have no idea where I'm going. I feel like the Mom of the car. When I was little, my mom would get all of us in the car, say she was taking us to dinner. She'd start driving, and somebody would ask where we were going, to which she would reply, "I don't know."

Right now, I don't know which way is up.

"Candy," Nick says, "they're not following us. Don't you think that's weird?"

Before I can reply, Christina says, "They don't have to follow us. They're tracking our phones. And as far as we know, this Hummer, too."

"Well then let's just throw the phones out the window, right?" Nick says.

I see a sign for a bus station. "I have a better idea," I say.

"What's that?" Christina asks.

"You'll see," I say, pulling the Hummer into a parking spot. "Do you know if there is any duct tape in here?" I ask.

"Are you kidding me?" Christina says. "If there isn't any in here, I probably have about ten rolls in my bag! Sean went crazy buying stuff." Her voice trails off. She reaches into her bag, grabs a roll, and hands it to me.

"Thanks," I say. "Now, we need to decide where to go."

"What is our plan?" Nick says.

"Well," I say, "we need to find out more about ViaLab. We need to find out who Mr. Z is, and I think I know where to start."

"Home?" Nick says.

"Home," I say.

We sneak around the back of the bus station, and I ask Christina and Nick for their phones. Nick hands his over first, and I begin wrapping duct tape around it until It's sticky on all sides. I reach up under the wheel well of a bus that has ATLANTA written on its LED destination sign and slap the phone there. Christina's phone gets a free trip to PORTLAND, and mine takes a ride to BOSTON.

"This is genius, Candy," Nick says.

"Thanks," I say, blushing. Christina looks at the ground.

"Where are you guys even from?" She asks.

I turn and point to the sign on the front of the bus behind me.

GRAND RAPIDS.

—

LOOKING BACK ON EVERYTHING, I see it probably wasn't the best idea to walk right into the lion's den, but this microphone is here to hear the truth of what happened, not what I wish had happened.

When it comes time to pay for our bus tickets, Christina realizes that the car keys weren't the only thing Sean had on him when he was killed. He had all of their cash as well. And even if we were dumb enough to use our cards, they were most likely null and void by now.

"How much money do we have?" I ask Nick. He fumbles through his pockets, pulling out his wallet. Looking up at the prices on the screen, he says, "Enough to get home. That's about it."

It comes to me then that I don't even know where

Christina and Sean are from. I don't know if it's the best time to bring Sean up, so I ask in another way. "Christina," I say, "Is there somewhere else you think we should go? Any ideas?"

Christina is swishing her yo-yo, looking forlorn. Looking up at me she says, "No, I don't have anyone. I don't have anything. Let's find these guys who put you up to this. I'm not going back to Vegas."

"Vegas?" I say, "is that where you're from?"

"Yes," she replies. "And it's Hell on Earth. Plus, I have way too many bad memories there." She looks away. "Good ones, too," she adds.

The man behind the counter is waving me over. I walk over to him.

"Hey listen, kid," he says. "Are you guys taking the bus or not? Driver's getting annoyed."

"Yes sir," I say. "Three tickets, please."

Nick walks over, hands over most of the cash, and we get on the bus.

16

CHECKING IN

CHRISTINA, NICK, AND I ARE SITTING IN THE BACK OF THE BUS, which, by the way, is the worst smelling part. No doubt the makeshift bathroom to many bums, the last couple rows smell like a basket of gym socks soaked in cat piss.

I'm starting to nod off when I hear Christina yelp. I jerk my head up, wipe the drool from the corner of my mouth.

"Oww!" She says, sucking her thumb. Blood is leaking from the tip. "I'm so stupid," she cries. Her yo-yo is lying on the floor.

"It's just a nervous thing," she says. "The yo-yo, I mean. I forgot to put my gloves on. I'm just so . . ."

"Rattled?" I say. "Can anyone blame you?"

"Definitely not," Nick says.

"Thanks," Christina says. "I'm okay. I just wish we had never gotten into this."

I think we all do. Even Nick, who thought he was fucking Batman at the start of all of this. And as Christina and Nick fall asleep next to me, I'm staring out the window, contemplating what to do next. But I know what I want to do first.

We're going to pay Todd and Ken a visit. It's time we get some answers.

—

I'M SITTING in Steve Hick's kitchen watching and waiting for his head to explode. In my mind, somewhere deep, I know this isn't real, but it's real on the surface. I try to scream for Steve to run. My mouth isn't working, or my voice isn't working, I'm not sure which.

Steve is sitting across from me, a hint of sadness in his eyes. He says, "In a way, I deserve this."

I try again to get him to act, to get out of the way of the bullet. It doesn't matter. He knows what's coming, even if I can't speak.

He says, "For my sins, I'll pay. And I'm so sorry you got mixed up in this."

And then the upper-half of his head is gone in a grotesque firework display.

I hear laughing behind me, and when I turn, I see Todd and Ken Carothers, high-fiving each other and clapping. Then out of nowhere, champagne flutes appear in their hands and they clink them together, smiling.

"Hey!" I shout. But of course, it's in silence. That's one of those dream things you just can't escape sometimes. My words are slaughtered in my throat by my own anxiety.

Suddenly, a massive scoreboard appears behind Todd and Ken. The brothers turn in anger as they watch the score for the AWAY side of the board increase by one point. Todd and Ken begin flipping furniture and shouting.

When I wake, the sun is high in the sky. Nick and Christina are playing cards.

"Where are we?" I ask.

Nick looks up from his hand. "Illinois," he says. "You slept a long time. We're not far from home."

My stomach is so empty it hurts. "I'm so hungry," I say. "And I have to use the bathroom."

Christina digs around in her bag and pulls out a protein bar. "Here," she says. "It should hold you over. We stopped at a rest area about an hour ago. Probably won't get another chance to go before we get there."

"Thanks," I say. I take a bite of the bar, which is dry and makes me feel like gagging. I choke it down anyway.

"Listen," Nick says, "I don't know what's going to happen when we get there." He pauses. "I know we have weapons, but I think you two should just let me confront them. I got us into this," he says.

"No," Christina says, "we're all in this together. And even if Candy is okay with letting you go alone, I'm not. These people killed Sean. Sean was my best friend, and more. I'm going."

When we arrive in Grand Rapids, we exit the bus, and Christina looks to me and Nick for reassurance.

"We're actually only a couple blocks from their house," Nick says. I find the bathroom, and we get going.

—

IT'S NOT LONG before we're standing in front of the doghouse in Todd and Ken's yard. Christina watches in amazement as we push the doghouse back and turn the wheel in the center of the water bowl.

"I've seen it all," she says as the ground opens up.

We walk down the hallway, and as the doghouse closes the hole above us, I hear the gunfire. Nick shoves me to the ground and pulls his pistol out of his pants. The alarm is blaring overhead, and smoke enters through the ventilation system. In a matter of seconds, I can't see a foot in front of my own face. Nick is crawling on his belly as he grabs my hand and pulls me along, letting me know to follow him. Down on the ground, I can see a straight path in front of my face, enough to tell which way I'm going.

The gunfire grows louder, but none of us have been hit. I can't even hear any bullets ricocheting off the walls. Nick fires a couple of rounds in the general direction of our attackers. He waits, fires again.

Something strange happens. The sound of the gunfire actually warps, slows. And after a loud electric popping sound, it stops.

On the floor, Nick is motioning for Christina and me to keep down. We wait for a long moment. The alarm has stopped, and the smoke is thinning. Nick is crawling forward. I follow him, and Christina follows me. When we reach the end of the hallway, I see where the gunfire sound was coming from. A large speaker is sitting on a table and going straight through the horn in the center is a bullet.

"They're not here," Nick says.

"How do you know?" Christina asks, her voice shaky.

"They set up a makeshift alarm through the PA system," Nick says. "They rigged a smoke machine and this gun sound file to play at the same time. This is an elaborate trick. They wouldn't go through all this trouble if they were here."

"We need to look around anyway," I say.

"Of course," Nick says.

We search the building thoroughly. It's Christina who finds the information we need.

"Guys," she says, pointing ahead.

"What did you find?" I ask. But then I see it. The desktop on the computer is open to an email.

I HAVE FORWARDED your plane tickets. We have terminated the experiment. When you arrive in Vegas, meet me below the Double Down. We are so much closer to the ultimate goal. These people will pay for what they've done to us.

-Z

17

WINDOW SHOPPING

CHRISTINA STARES AT THE COMPUTER SCREEN LONG AFTER we've all read the message there. I'm not sure what exactly it is that terrifies her about Vegas, but it's behind her eyes right now like a demon trying to escape. After some time, rather than scream, or break down in tears, she laughs. She laughs hard.

"Christina?" I say, hesitantly.

She's still laughing. I guess I missed the joke.

"Hey," Nick says, touching Christina's shoulder. She turns and looks Nick in the eyes. And then she begins to cry.

"I don't know if I can go back there," she cries. I move towards her to comfort her, but she backs away, wiping her nose with the back of her hand. "Why would they be there of all places? It's like the universe is trying to fuck with me!"

"Well," Nick says. "It's obvious that this whole thing is bigger than we understand. We started out here, and you started out there, but the people who put us up to this know each other somehow. I guess it's not too much of a stretch that they would meet up."

Christina knows this, I can see it in her face, she's being

rhetorical. But there's something about Vegas that terrifies her, and I'm not sure I want to know what it is.

"How are we even going to get there?" Christina asks. "We don't have any money. I think it may be time to hang it up."

"Christina," I say. "With all due respect, you only started saying this when you realized we'd have to go to Vegas. What happened to avenging Sean's death?"

"Well," she replies, "am I wrong? How are we going to get there?"

I lean against the wall behind me, my ass sliding to the floor. My brain feels like mush. I don't know what to think about anything anymore. I look up at Nick, who also looks lost in thought. And then it hits me.

"How do you guys feel about breaking the law?" I ask.

Christina laughs again.

—

So, here's the deal: my dad owns a Ford dealership. And as much as I hate to do it, I know he's got the best insurance possible. We're going to steal a car. Of course, Nick loves the idea. He's not my dad's biggest fan.

We gather as many supplies as we can from the bunker before going. We've got water, food, and a small amount of cash now. With a vehicle, we can definitely make it to Vegas. There's only one problem: It's about a twenty-seven-hour drive to Vegas from here. Even if we drive non-stop, rotating drivers and taking turns sleeping, that's still over an entire day on the road. But unless someone shits out some plane tickets, it's our only choice.

A few hours later, we're drinking coffee in the Starbucks across the road from Tran Ford. Nick is using a pair of binoculars he snatched from Todd and Ken's underground lair. At least, that's what Nick calls it.

"I see your dad, Candy," Nick says. "Do you want to see?"

I didn't even realize how hard I was biting my lip until I tasted the blood. I reach for the binoculars. And there he is, completely unaware of what is about to happen to him. Please understand that I have nothing against my dad. I love him, but this is the only thing I can think of right now. You might be wondering what happened to our personal vehicles. Well, Nick's is at the airport across town where we would have to pay to pick it up—and it's been there a LONG time. Remember, this was supposed to be covered by 'Mr. Z' and gang. Not to mention, I highly doubt either of our vehicles would even make it across the state line. You can forget about a twenty-seven-hour trip one way.

It's not happening. No, I've got my eyes set on a fast one. Right out front, is a brand-new Ford GT. According to my dad, it tops out around 215 miles per hour. I'll try to be careful with it. Maybe I can return it at some point.

The dealership closes in thirty minutes. Another thirty minutes after that should be plenty of time for everyone to be gone from the building. We've got some time to waste and I want to ask Christina the question so bad.

"What are you so afraid of in Las Vegas?" I blurt.

Christina looks like I just punched her in the ovaries. "Well, I," she stutters. Her hands open and close and she reaches nervously for her yo-yo. "Damnit. I didn't want to have to go into this," she says.

"You don't have to," Nick says.

"No, I do," she says. "I need to talk about it, I think. As much as I don't want to. The thing is, Sean and I were kind of roped into this whole ordeal after we did something wrong. Something *very* wrong."

Us too, I'm thinking. *Us too.*

Christina continues, "Sean and I were not bad people before all of this. It's just crazy how it all happened." She's full-on clutching the yo-yo now, red lines digging into her palm where the razor cuts against her skin. Tears fill her eyes. "It was so. . . fast," she whispers.

"What was so fast?" I ask, gently.

"Everything," Christina whimpers. Blood drips onto the table from her severed palm. "He was crossing the road when I looked down for a fraction of a second. I'll never forget the sound of the screeching tires. I'll never forget the *thud* of his small body slamming into our car. I'll never forget the sight of his one sneaker flying through the air. He was only *four years old*."

"Oh my God," I say. "That's so awful."

"And then," Christina continues, "we got out of the car to check on him, and I found a red yo-yo on the ground next to his body."

It all makes sense now. Christina didn't add razors to the yo-yo to turn it into a weapon. She added them for self-injury. For penitence.

"What happened then?" Nick asks.

"Then," Christina says, "these two guys pulled up in a cop car, put us in the back, and took us to what they said was the station. It wasn't. It was another place altogether. They proceeded to tell us how they could get us out of this mess. I think you know what happened next."

"We sure do," I say. And then Nick and I tell Christina our story up until the part where we met her and Sean.

"This is insane," she says. "This whole thing."

"Yep," I say. "And it's just getting worse."

—

I KNOW where my dad hides the spare key to the dealership. It opens the maintenance entrance, but it will still get us inside the building. Once we're inside, the security alarm starts chiming. I run to the panel and enter the code (it has always been my birthday). I push the touchscreen on the ADT panel (fun fact I learned from my Last Podcast on the Left obsession—Dennis Rader, the BTK killer, worked as an ADT technician), and my code is wrong.

Since when? I start to panic, as the timer counts down 10...9...8... *oh my god oh my god oh my god.*

And I *know* my dad gets alerts on his phone when the alarm is triggered. Okay. What else could it be? My parents' wedding date? What was it again...? 0924.

Wrong. Damn! At this point the alarm is already screaming. I dash to the office and grab the keys for the display vehicle. The label reads F250. So much for 215 MPH.

"Someone is coming!" Nick shouts. I toss him the keys and point to the cobalt blue pickup in the front display window. As Nick and Christina climb into the cab of the F250, I spare a quick glance at the photo on my dad's desk. Our little family, before all of this. Seemingly happy. And when I turn to the leave the office, I find a pistol in my face.

18

THRILLER

As a kid, I always felt like my dad would do anything for me. And I mean absolutely anything. I can remember vividly the time I was convinced Michael Jackson's character from the 'Thriller' video was living in my closet. I expressed my concerns to my dad, who took watch in my room all night (meaning until I fell asleep, and then returning right before I woke) with a baseball bat in his lap, just in case MJ decided to come out and say 'Hi.' It sounds funny now, but at the time, it was fucking terrifying.

All throughout my childhood I enjoyed the comfort and protection my dad provided. I did not truly want for anything, and I knew my dad would never hurt me. Which is why it's a strange feeling having him tell me to put my hands up slowly, or he will blow my fucking brains out.

"Dad," I say. "It's me. . . it's just me." My vocal cords grate like a sandpaper dildo, but at least he lowers the gun, and I no longer have to look down the barrel, wondering what the chances are of the gun failing to kill me and only severely maiming me for life. Drinking liquified tater-tot-hot-dish through a straw until I get tired of living and step off a tall ledge at the age of thirty-five.

"C-Candy?" My dad stammers. "What the hell are you doing? Where have you been? I thought you and Nick were—"

"Dad, if you could just disable the alarm system, we can talk," I say.

"It's too late," he says. "I already got an alert saying police have dispatched."

The engine on the big Ford roars. Nick's warning.

"I can't explain it that fast, dad," I say.

"Try," he says.

"I just need you to trust me," I plead.

"Are you in trouble, Candy?" My dad asks. "Tell me what it is, I can help you."

"The only way you can help me right now," I say, "is to let me go."

"Not unless you explain what's going on, damnit!" He cries.

Police lights flash down the road.

"I'm sorry," I say. And then I turn and run towards the truck. I climb into the passenger seat and steal one last glance in my dad's direction. He just stands there, dumbfounded, his gun limply hanging in his hand. And as the police draw nearer, I see my dad raise the gun in our direction and fire twice. The glass in front of us shatters, and Nick drives the truck through the window and out onto the street.

—

I'M NOT sure how long, but it's a good while before anyone speaks. I find it hard to process what just occurred. The look of my dad with tears in his eyes, it's just too much. Anyways. Twenty-seven hours of driving. This is going to be hell. Everyone is exhausted, but Nick offers to drive until he no longer feels it's safe at which point he says he will 'lie down across the back seat and die.'

Christina sleeps quietly behind us as we cross state lines. Nick yawns loudly.

"Hey," I say, "let me drive. You're about to pass out over there."

"I'm okay," he says. "Just talk to me. I'll be fine."

I realize that I don't even know what Nick and I would talk about anymore. We've been doing this for what seems like forever now. There hasn't been time to even have a conversation. I open my mouth to speak. I've got nothing specific to say, just whatever verbal diarrhea spills out will do just fine. But before I can say anything, Nick says, "I want you to know that I'm sorry for being such a piece of shit."

"What do you mean?" I ask.

"You know what I mean," he says. "I get these feelings that I can't explain. I do things that I can't remember doing. Like, you know, with Todd's clone. It was like a dream. I saw him walking, then I saw him dead on the ground. I just don't like who I am sometimes. And I know you don't, either."

I honestly don't know what to say to Nick. This all catches me off-guard. If Nick was feeling a loss of sanity, or a loss of control, why wouldn't he just tell me before now?

Nick continues, "I've just been going along for the ride, trying to protect you. Back in Tallahassee, when I went back for that guy's wife, it was because she *saw* you. I didn't enjoy doing what I did. I know you probably think I did. And we were so close to home, but now we're driving an entire day in the opposite direction. When does it end?"

I don't know the answer to that. I don't even know what we're doing anymore, most of the time. I think hard before answering.

"I guess it ends when we figure out what ViaLab is and get these people to leave us alone," I say.

"Or when we die," he says.

———

YEAH. . . so, I refuse to bore you to death with the details of the trip. I can tell you this: it fucking sucks. Just over an entire day of riding in a truck with two other people cramped together like sardines is not that exciting. Unfortunately for Christina, it only makes sense to have her drive when we get just outside of Vegas. Luckily, I think it was therapeutic for her to tell us the reason she wanted to avoid this place, and she seems to be holding herself together better than I was expecting.

"So," Christina says, "the Double Down is a bar and music venue for local punks. The email said they would meet 'below the Double Down,' and I know the place has a basement where people can play pool and things like that. That would be my first place to check."

"We don't know when they were supposed to meet though," Nick says. "They could be long gone by now."

"We knew this when we agreed to come out here," I say. "But it's all we have. We have to try to find them. Someone there will know something."

I glance at the clock on the dash. 10:30 PM. Prime time for the shithole known as the Double Down. We might as well go there right now. Even though we all gave up our cell-phones, we still have our guns, and I doubt a place like this checks for those.

—

I WAS WRONG.

—

THE NEXT PART is a bit hazy for me. In part because of the massive amounts of alcohol in my bloodstream, in part because of my head injury. From what I can recall, we make it into the Double Down with no problems. As Heather Wolworth, I have no trouble ordering cheap drinks. Nick, Christina and I try to mingle among the crowd as we search for the entrance to the basement, but among these spiky-haired, leather-clad folks, we stick out like a hard dick. It doesn't take too long before we're pulled aside and asked a few questions. A fine gentleman with the words 'FUCK YOU' tattooed on his knuckles says he needs to know what our business here is.

"Just trying to have a good time," I say. Except my words come out more like 'jus tryna hava goodime.'

"Yeah, sure," the guy says. "And I'm Mary-fuckin'-Poppins. What is your *business* here?"

And Nick blurts it out. I don't blame him, I'm not sure how else we were supposed to ask it, and this guy seems to know what the deal is anyway.

"We're here to see Mr. Z," Nick says.

"Follow me," the guy says.

—

MR. FUCK KNUCKLES leads us to the back door, where were we are searched. In retrospect, I think it would have been a great idea to have one of us hold back outside or something. Anything other than the three of us walking like lambs to the slaughter with our weapons confiscated.

"They're all packing!" Says a tall man who smells like a leather couch.

"I figured," says Fuck Knuckles. "You know what to do."

And that's when Nick does something incredibly ballsy, and incredibly dumb. As leather couch guy reaches for his gun, Nick smashes his head forward as hard as he can, crashing into the guy's face. I can hear the crack of the bridge of his nose, followed by shouting and cursing. The group of men lunge towards Nick, fists flying. Christina is screaming, and Nick holds up his arms in self-defense. A short man from the back of the pack walks up, wielding a baseball bat. Everything happens so fast, but what happens is Nick ducks at just the right time, and I catch a bat to the side of the head like a closet Michael Jackson.

19

DEUS EX MEXICANA

WHEN I REGAIN CONSCIOUSNESS, I'M LYING ON MY SIDE, FEET and hands bound together. It's dark and cramped, and my face is inches away from Nick's ass. The bounce and sway beneath me, coupled with the distinct sound of tires slowly crunching on gravel tells me I'm in the trunk of a car.

Very little light comes through from the outside. That's how I know I'm at the mercy of Nick's gastrointestinal system.

"Nick," I whisper. "Nick, can you hear me?"

Nick doesn't reply. I nudge him in the back with my knee.

"Umph," Nick grunts.

"Wake up," I plead, pushing the back of his head with my foot.

Nick draws in a rushing breath of air, attempts to sit up, and slams his head into the roof of the trunk. "Where am I?" He says.

"Universal Studios," I say. "This is the one where you ride in the back of a homicidal maniac's trunk before they throw you in a hole in the ground."

Nick is silent for a few moments. Then he utters one word: "Shit."

"Where is Christina?" I ask.

Nick doesn't respond.

The crunching beneath the tires is slowing.

"Nick?" I say.

"I don't know where she is," he says. "They took her somewhere. They said they were going to have *fun* with her."

Even though I'm sweating my non-existent balls off in this hundred-degree trunk in the Nevada heat, my blood runs cold at this. The car comes to a stop. A door opens and shuts. Boots on gravel. A cellphone rings.

"Yeah," a gruff voice says. "Well, no shit." There's a long pause as feet crunch on the ground. "Well this isn't exactly rocket science," the man says. "You put a bullet in their heads, throw them in the pit."

Nick is shaking next to me. Everything we've been working towards is about to end in this dried-up wasteland. Sweat runs down into my eyes.

"I'm not ready to die," Nick whispers. It's the sincerest thing I've ever heard him say, and I wonder if the same is true for me, if I really even care anymore. Honestly, I'm more interested in saving Christina from whatever terrible fate she's facing than worrying about my own death. And just like in the beginning of the story, I'm sure you're thinking I'm just this emo, whiny little girl. What's scary is I'm not whining, just being honest with myself.

The sounds of gravel crunching grow closer and closer until finally, the trunk opens. I'm blinded by the desert sun shining high in the sky. One of the goons from the Double Down stares at us from behind expensive sunglasses. A scar runs the length of the left side of his face, no doubt some form of punishment, considering his line of work.

"Who wants to go first?" he asks.

"I'll go first," I say. "If you answer a question for me."

"I'm waiting," the man says.

I swallow. This isn't one of my brightest moments. My voice shakes a bit as I say, "When you have Mr. Z's dick in the back of your throat, does he at least play with your hair?"

The man's face grows incredibly tense as the corners of his mouth twitch. His tongue moves across the inside of his mouth like someone trying to clean popcorn from the front of their teeth. "You know," he says. "I'm going to let you go second. Because I'll need more time with you. And I'm going to have fun. And I will *not* play with your hair."

I'm panicking. I can't move much at all, aside from flopping like a fish on a chopping block. The man reaches into the trunk and grabs Nick with both hands. "Come on, big guy," he says. "Don't make this harder than it has to be." As Nick is dragged from the trunk, his eyes say it all.

Goodbye.

The man with the scar on his face turns to me. He says, "This here pit is known to have the worst this desert has to offer. All types of predators: rattlesnakes, mountain lions, bobcats, scorpions. Hell, the biggest fuckin' spiders you'll ever see. Now, I'm gonna do right by your friend here—as right as I can, you understand, given my instructions—that is to say that he will be dead *before* I drop him to the bottom. Which, by the way, is only really far enough to break your legs. Maybe a couple ribs." The man smiles. He says, "I just want you to know what that little comment cost you. Because you won't be so lucky. With you, I won't waste a bullet. You'll be alive when you land in that fucking hole. And you will scream. God, will you scream. But you won't be heard by anything except for the beasts who will hear your cries of distress as a dinner bell." The man lays Nick flat on his face in the hot sand, points a gun at the back of his head. He continues, "Now, I could give you this whole spiel about how I'm going to make you watch, but the good lord knows I can't force you to do that. But I can force you to do a lot of others things. You'll see. So, if you need to close your eyes, you go ahead. Just as long as you know you're next."

My mom always said my mouth would get me into trouble one day. I wonder if this is what she meant.

And folks, I'd be lying to you if I said I didn't close my eyes. I've seen enough death. And my own heart nearly stopped when I heard the echoing gunshot.

—

I CAN'T SEEM to open my eyes. I don't want to see the creep standing over me, waiting to do whatever he plans to do to me. I can hear shuffling feet. Grunting. Panting. Tears streak my face as I fight back the urge to vomit. Were we wrong to try to track these people down?

No. They were going to kill us either way. We did the best we could. Christina, I'm so sorry. I'm sorry we got you to come with us. I'm sorry we couldn't save you.

Still not daring to look at Nick's lifeless body, I open my eyes and glance around the trunk for something to use as a weapon. There's nothing. Nothing at all.

Just me and my stupid flabby ass.

And then I hear the sound of Nick's body being dragged into the pit, the dead weight sliding along the gravel and sand. I hear a grunting noise, and then, seconds later, a sickening *splat.*

The footsteps come closer as the man returns to collect me. My fight-or-flight instincts kick in, and I finally pop my head out of the vehicle. I see the trail of blood leading to the pit where Nick's body was dragged after being shot. Except there's a problem with that. Nick's body is still lying face-down in the sand.

A familiar face pops from the side of the trunk. "He so scared, he pass out! Piss himself too! I don' blame him though," the voice says.

My bindings are cut, and a friendly hand helps pull me out of the trunk. "Now, is time to go save tu amiga," says The Mexican. "A lot of people going to pay."

20

LOAD UP ON GUNS, BRING YOUR
FRIENDS

I'M STRUGGLING TO COMPREHEND WHAT'S HAPPENING. JUST FOR
the record, Nick is *not* dead, and I'm suddenly *not* about to die.

Well that's a relief.

"What are you doing here?" I ask. "How did you,
I mean—"

"Is not meant to be for you to die today, Candy," says The
Mexican. "I am not bad man, and money is not worth what
they ask of me. So, I stopped the man."

"But why are you here in Vegas?" I ask.

"Is where they wanted me," he says. "Is where they want
everyone who work for them."

"Who are they?" I ask. "Who is Mr. Z?"

The Mexican lowers his head. "I don't know that," he
says. Nudging Nick with his foot, he says, "Except for where
we can most likely find tu amiga."

Nick stirs on the ground.

"Where is that?" I ask.

"Well," The Mexican says, "I'm not a hundred percen'
sure, but I think she might be at this place call ViaLab."

Nick bolts upright. "What the hell happened?" He asks.

"He saved us," I say, gesturing towards our silver-toothed friend. I turn back to The Mexican. "Why do you think she's at ViaLab?" I ask.

The Mexican takes the cowboy hat off of his head, fanning himself with it. He spits on the ground before saying, "Because that's where Mr. Z is."

"Have you met him?" I ask. "What does he look like?"

"No," he says. "Only talk on phone."

"If you work for him, why are you helping us?" Nick asks, brushing dirt and gravel from his clothes and hair.

"I find out what Mr. Z really does," The Mexican says, "kidnapping. Murdering. No honor in it. Money not worth it, man. I help you now."

"We appreciate it," I say. "But what did you *think* Mr. Z was doing?"

"Honestly," The Mexican says. "I only ever run drugs in the ice-cream truck. Sometimes people, or other cargo. But now they want to put people in holes and put holes in people."

"What do you know about ViaLab?" Nick asks.

The Mexican shrugs. "Not much, really," he says. "But I do know where it is."

"And how to get in?" Nick asks.

"Si," The Mexican replies.

—

WE PILE BACK into the car. This time however, Nick and I

don't have to ride in the trunk. And for the second time, The Mexican acts as our chauffeur.

"Where exactly are we headed?" I ask. "We're not ready to just storm into ViaLab. We don't even have any weapons or anything."

"I take you to Mr. Z's private armory. He has everything there."

Folks, I'm nervous. I don't know what's going to happen next, and I'm afraid to find out. But I have to. *We* have to. Because it's the right thing to do. And because I don't have a choice. And when I think back on how this all started, it's hard to believe how much we've been through. All because Nick killed Todd's clone. Even that statement itself sounds crazy.

Nick and I, Christina and Sean, and who knows how many other individuals or groups were blackmailed into murdering certain individuals. All of whom seem to be connected back to the same place—ViaLab.

—

"WE'RE HERE!" The Mexican announces, jolting me from a sleep I didn't know I was taking part in. I look around and see a small, inconspicuous storage unit directly in front of the car.

"Will anyone be here?" Nick asks. "Guards? Anyone?"

"Normally, si," said The Mexican. "Right now, everyone leave for ViaLab. To guard Mr. Z, I guess. And tu amiga."

We get out of the car and The Mexican presses the bracelet on his wrist to the receiver on the door frame. The little light turns from red to green, and a small beep lets us know that his key fob has been accepted.

The door to the unit begins rolling upward, and already, I can see the plethora of weaponry available to choose from. Rack after rack of all kinds of guns: pistols, rifles, shotguns, submachine guns, you name it.

"Why would Mr. Z risk storing all of this here?" I ask. "Why not keep it somewhere safer?"

"He owns this place," The Mexican says. "Can't get much safer."

"Does he own ViaLab?" Nick asks.

"He does by now," The Mexican says, before stepping over the threshold into the storage unit. Nick and I follow him.

After a few moments, Nick says, "Holy shit, this is amazing."

"Of course you would say that," I say. "You might want to wipe the drool from your mouth."

"Let's try to hurry," The Mexican says.

I find a tall storage locker in the back of the unit, filled with leather jackets. When I take one down, I see why. The inside of the jacket is lined with built-in holsters for both guns and knives, and pouches for extra ammunition. I find one that fits my frame and put it on. I look over at Nick and see him checking himself out in the reflection from a gun cabinet. He's got ammo everywhere it can be held, and so many guns crossing on his back that he's slightly hunched over.

Once we are loaded down with all the weapons we can manage, we fill the vehicle with as many large guns as we can and close the unit. Somehow, none of us see the security cameras that watched our every move.

—

"NOT TOO FAR NOW," The Mexican says, after we've driven for a while.

I'm just looking out the window, watching the desert scenery pass by in rapid succession. Wondering if I'm going to die today. And then, as if he was reading my mind, The Mexican says, "You know we could die today. In fact, we probably will."

"Why are you doing this, then?" Nick asks.

The Mexican shrugs. "I've got nothing better to do," he says, with a hoarse laugh. He then begins coughing, and when he wipes his mouth, I see blood. "Sorry about that," he says, noticing me watching him. "I guess I should add that I am very sick."

"I'm sorry," I say. "Cancer?"

The Mexican shrugs and says no more on the subject. His indifference scares me, and I can't help but feel a twinge of pain for him. But that's how some people are, either too afraid to let others see their true emotions, or worse, too afraid to let themselves feel them.

We ride then, mostly in silence for the rest of the trip to ViaLab's headquarters.

In my head, the same thoughts are playing over and over.

We're coming for you, Christina.
We're coming for you, Mr. Z.

21

BACK DOOR MAN

I want to thank you for listening to my story this far. We're getting close to the end, the part that's so important. So, please, ladies and gentlemen of the jury, hear my testimony. And for God's sake, please pay attention.

"We're getting close!" Shouts The Mexican.

"How are we going to get in?" Nick asks.

The Mexican pulls the car to the side of the road. "I have idea," he says.

—

"Are you sure this is going to work?" I ask. "There has to be a better way."

"Is only way," The Mexican replies. "They scan badge, they look in car. I can say I am bringing guns for Mr. Z, and you can join me in car after gate."

I look and see the lever that lets the trunk open into the backseat. "Are you ready?" He asks us.

"As ready as we'll ever be," Nick says.

"Yeah," I agree. "Let's do it." And then The Mexican closes the trunk, and Nick and I find ourselves in darkness again. Only, this time we're not tied up. We may still be on our way to our deaths though.

We're only a few miles from ViaLab's headquarters, but the drive feels maddeningly long. I'm starting to wonder how we could be so stupid. I'm wondering how we're going to have even the slightest chance of survival. But then the vehicle slows, and The Mexican's window begins to roll down.

"Hola, amigo," I hear another man's voice say.

"Hello, friend," The Mexican says.

"What's your business here today?" The guard asks.

"Special delivery for Mr. Z," The Mexican says. "He wan' a lot of guns, I bring a lot of guns."

The man barks a laugh. "I hear that!" He says. "You'd think they were preparing for a war."

A beeping sound tells me the guard scanned The Mexican's ID badge.

"Go on ahead," the guard says.

"Gracias," calls The Mexican, and we're moving again.

After a moment, The Mexican says, "You two can come up here now."

Nick pulls the lever leading into the backseat, and we climb through the open hole.

"We will pull around the back of the building," The Mexican says. "Jus' lay low until I say. And be ready to start shooting, jus' in case. After that, jus' follow me, and I'll take you straight to tu amiga."

"This is crazy," I say, "we're going to die."

"They won't be expecting anything," The Mexican says.

The car comes to a stop in front of a brick wall. Glancing around, I can see cameras on every corner. The Mexican jumps out and begins to sling gun after gun over his shoulder. Nick and I begin doing the same.

"Okay friends," The Mexican says. "If you follow me closely, we shoul' be okay. I know where they will be come from, okay?"

"Okay," Nick and I say in unison. But I don't feel okay. The Mexican mutters under his breath, signs a cross over his face and chest, and begins walking toward the building. His key card scans just fine, and we're inside. I'm expecting alarms to wail, red flashing lights. Instead, I hear pleasant elevator music.

"How have they not seen us on the cameras?" I ask.

"I know the guy who work this shift," The Mexican says. "He don' do his job, man. Looks at porn and shit."

"Oh," I say. "Well . . . good."

And then the sirens and red flashing lights begin, while we stand in the back entrance of ViaLab with an arsenal on our backs. We look like a cross between *Rambo* and *Ghostbusters*.

"Follow me!" The Mexican shouts as he ducks into a room on the right. We dive behind a desk in the far corner of the room. It's impossible to think clearly with the alarms wailing like newborn babies. Red lights strobing the walls. But with my back against the desk, I see that the wall facing us is lined with computer monitors. On the monitor closest, I see three guys in beige jumpsuits, each sitting in a different corner of a small padded room, staring at the floor.

There's shouting from the hallway.

The Mexican waves his hands at us and begins crawling into the adjoining room. Nick and I follow. In the doorway between the rooms, The Mexican stops, and I realize what he's doing before he even says it.

"I'm gon' start shooting," he says. "And they'll funnel through the doors in this room," he points to the right. "And that room," he points to the left. "And we'll gun them all down." Without any further warning, The Mexican begins firing.

—

I NEARLY FREEZE when the first security guard walks through the room on the left. But when I see his gun raise and point at my face, I find my courage. I pull the submachine gun I'm wielding up and pull the trigger.

Click. It's jammed. I squint and recoil, waiting for the bullets to tear through me, but then a deafening *pow* on my right saves my life. Nick lowers the *Dirty Harry* style revolver.

"Thanks," I say. He takes the gun from me and slams his hand on the magazine. When he hands it back to me, he kisses me, which catches me completely off-guard.

"What is it?" He asks.

The Mexican takes out two more guards with a single shotgun blast.

"What is what?" I ask.

Nick shoots another man entering the room on the left. The man grabs his chest and trips forward over the first body on the floor and slams his face into the corner of a desk.

Nick, looking at the man impaled on the desk, he says, "Why were you looking at me like that?"

Because I haven't felt that way in a long time.

"It was just nice," I say. "For you to kiss me like that."

"Wait!" The Mexican shouts. The shooting has stopped and the guards have finally gotten smart enough to stop toppling to their death.

Simultaneously, the three of us duck to the floor as giant holes fill the walls. Bullets spray angrily above and behind us, smashing into everything. The Mexican begins crawling on his belly until he's in the center of the room. The bullets fly around him as he reaches behind his back and pulls a grenade out of a little pouch. He looks over at us slowly.

"No!" I demand.

"I knew I wasn' going to survive this," The Mexican says. "No way, José." He smiles a little, then says, "Don't let this be for nothing." And then he's gone. And as the multiple guards in the hallway shoot him down, I can almost hear The Mexican laughing one final time, just before the grenade takes out the entire hallway.

22

SLEEPER

THE SHORT VERSION: OUCH.

The long version: the grenade that takes out The Mexican and the entire group of guards also wipes out half of the rooms on this side of the building. The force of the blast slams my body against the wall of monitors behind me, chunks of glass hit me all over my body and face, a shard of metal goes through my palm—a makeshift stigmata.

I scream in agony as the burning metal sears through the skin on my right hand. Looking around, I see Nick lying on the floor, covering his ears. He's surrounded by a small fire.

"Shit!" He yells, rolling away from the flames. He jumps to his feet and before I can protest, snatches the piece of metal, causing a stream of blood to pour from my open palm. I scream in pain.

"I'm sorry," he says, "it had to come out." He takes a bandana out of his ammo pouch. "I thought I'd wear this like some kind of badass soldier or something," he says, wrapping it around my hand, "but I think I found a better use for it."

"I think the crazy bastard got them," I say. I'm trying to ignore the chunks of bloody flesh coating the walls. "A lot of them, anyway," I add.

"We have to keep moving if we want to find Christina," Nick says. "I'm sure more are coming." He's picking little pieces of glass out of my hair.

"I hate this," I say. I can't stop the tears. I can't help but remember the fact that I wouldn't be in this predicament if it wasn't for Nick.

"I know," Nick says, pulling me up by my good hand. "Come on, it's almost over."

I get to my feet and just stand there, shaking. I say, "I don't see why so many people had to die for this. These guards, they—"

"Know exactly what goes on here," Nick says.

"We don't even know what goes on here," I reply.

"How does it feel?" Nick asks, eyeing my bloody hand.

"It feels wonderful, Nick," I say. "Like a kiss from an angel."

"Can you still shoot with that hand?" He asks.

"If I have to," I say. "But I can try the other."

"No," he says. "You'll shoot me by accident or something. Just stay close to me and let's hope you don't have to worry about it."

He starts walking towards the far side of the room, and I follow him. It's hard not to look at the scattered human remains, and I'm struggling to find my happy place.

"Here," Nick says. "This door will get us to the main room."

"How do you know?" I ask.

Nick frowns and says, "Isn't it obvious? It just makes sense." He shrugs.

I follow him through the door, and immediately I see two more armed men jogging in our direction. I reach for my gun, but Nick guns them both down before I can even wrap my hand around the grip. The room we've entered is a vast rectangle with high ceilings and dozens of doors, each room no doubt the vessel for various experiments to be carried out.

"Which way do we go now, genius?" I ask Nick.

"Let's just start picking rooms," he says. "It's the only plan we have."

We walk to the door on the far right, and then I realize something: We don't have a key card. The Mexican had one, but it's now most likely ash in the air.

The red light above the door stares down at us, daring us to try to enter.

"The guards!" I nearly scream. I jog over to the two guards lying on the ground, snatching the access card from one of their belt clips.

When I return to the door with the card, I hastily press it against the reader, the same way The Mexican did outside.

A loud beep. **Access Denied.**

I swipe it again. **Access Denied.**

The alarms are still wailing, my ears are still ringing, and I'm starting to wish Mr. Z would just come out here right now and confront me himself. I'm sick of this bullshit cat and mouse thing he's doing. If he wants me dead so badly, he needs to come down here and show me how much.

—

"WHAT DO WE DO?" I ask Nick.

Nick glances around the room. "They can't *all* be locked, can they?" he says. "Let's just look to make sure. This can't be the end of the line."

Please let it be the end of the line, a tired voice deep inside says.

"Okay," I say. "Yeah. I'll take the left side of the room."

I begin checking all the doors, each one just the same as the last. No window looking in, and a red light above the door denying my entry. I slide down to the floor, feeling defeated. "Come out here, motherfucker!" I yell. "I'm done with this game!"

"Candy!" Nick yells. "Over here!"

Somehow, Nick has found the only door in the room with a green light above it.

"What's in there, you think?" I ask him.

"There's no telling.," he replies. "After you."

Nick, always the gentleman.

When I approach the door, it opens automatically. The room is lit with harsh white lights, more computer monitors line the walls. In the center of the room is a computer terminal with a large, red flashing button. It seems to draw me in like a fly to hot garbage. Without even thinking, I push the button.

The lights dim and a video begins playing on the computer screens, connected side by side forming one massive display. On the screen flashes a message in white letters on a black background.

Experiment #298401C – Understanding Conscience, Guilt.

The screen goes black for a moment, and then we see Christina sitting in a chair in a room a lot like the one Nick and I are currently in. On the screen, two men walk in, their backs to the camera. Christina cries softly, asking when she can go, asking what they want from her.

We just want you to watch a little movie, one of the men says. He takes an object out of his pocket and sets it on the table.

That's it? Christina asks.

That's it, the man says. The two men turn and exit the room. It was only a glimpse, just a half-second, but I knew the two men were Todd and Ken Carothers.

—

ONCE CHRISTINA IS ALONE in the room, the 'movie' begins playing. It starts with footage from a small boy's birthday party, the camera working its way around the room, catching glimpses of the boy and all of his friends playing.

Christina is weeping. She's asking for someone to please stop the tape.

"What the hell is this?" I say, "where is she?"

"I don't know," Nick says.

But we can't stop watching.

The video moves on to surveillance footage from a streetlight camera. I'm gripping the edge of my seat so hard my fingers have gone cold.

Please, Christina begs. *Please, no more.*

On the screen, a small boy comes into view.

"Oh no," I say, my voice cracks.

Nick is frantic, trying to find any way to stop the video feed. He starts smashing computers and monitors, but the video keeps playing.

A car comes into the bottom portion of the screen. The video slows down just before Christina's car runs the little boy over like an out-of-place traffic cone. Christina is screaming now as the footage starts over.

And over.

And over.

My heart is beating furiously. The little object that flies off screen just after the boy was crushed is the same object sitting on the table in front of Christina.

Christina gets up out of the chair and bangs on the door. She asks for someone to let her out.

Please, just let me out.

The footage of Christina and the 'movie' fast-forwards then. On the bottom of the screen, a timer flashes. Hours go by.

Days.

I'm full-on sobbing now. "Please make it stop," I say to no one in particular. I know Nick can't help me, though he's trying.

Suddenly the video stops fast-forwarding and the audio returns. This time, after the video shows the small boy being struck by the car, the footage changes to something new: a news clip. The boy's mother cries and asks who would do such a thing?

Christina walks over to the table in the center of the room. She picks up her yo-yo with the little razor blades built in, chucks it at the screen. It bounces violently to the floor. The video keeps playing.

Christina gets quiet then. She calmly hangs her head, picks up the yo-yo, and sits in the chair. She takes a deep breath, sniffling quietly. And then she takes the sharp edge of the yo-yo and runs it down the length of both of her forearms.

Nick and I sit in silence as Christina twitches one last time, an eternal sleeper.

23

ORIENTATION

THE VIDEO STOPS. I'VE NEVER SEEN NICK SO ANGRY THE whole time we've known each other. Slamming his fists on the counter, he screams, "YOU WEREN'T SUPPOSED TO KILL HER YOU STUPID FUCKS!"

I never knew he cared so much about Christina.

"Nick," I say, "they don't care what you think. Don't you see what this is? These people obviously get off on torturing people. There's no telling what all goes on here."

LET ME HELP YOU TO UNDERSTAND, a voice booms through the intercom system. I recognize the voice. How could I forget it? It tears at my very core every time Nick says something truly sweet (as rare as it is). In the back of my mind, I remember what I did with Todd. I remember that Nick still doesn't know.

"TODD!" Nick yells. "DON'T DO THIS!"

"What the fuck is going on?" I say.

The Power goes out.

—

AND STAYS OUT.

I call for Nick over and over, but he doesn't reply. Several moments go by, and I can't see a damn thing. Shuffling of feet and whispers surround me. I'm gripping my pistol tight.

"Nick!" I scream. "Where the hell are you?"

The screens come on and I jump, startled by the stark white background. Nearly blinded, I can barely make out the logo in the center of the screen.

ViaLab.

The screen changes to say: *Where your future is your past.*

Nick stands about five feet away from me, staring at the screen, arms folded.

The shot fades in on a man in a white lab coat. I recognize him immediately as Don Branson, the guy from Florida that Nick shot from the bushes. The one Nick and I thought was the clone of Ted Bundy.

Just saying that again makes me feel so fucking stupid.

Here at ViaLab, a much younger Don says, *we aim to do the impossible. Constantly evolving, our research has opened doors for us we never thought possible. And the best part? We always give back to the community.*

A second man pops up on the screen. *That's right,* Steve Hicks says, *all of our volunteers here at ViaLab are paid handsomely for their participation. And they all leave unharmed with smiles on their faces.*

"Like Christina did?" I scream over the video.

—*even covering the cost of college for the less-than-fortunate family,* says a man whom I don't recognize. The screen shows couples holding their babies in a waiting lounge. A doctor checking a baby's ears. A family holding a massive check in front of the ViaLab headquarters doors. The couple, I also recognize. The parents of Todd and Ken.

Twitching at the back of my mind, something says, *Of course. You knew, didn't you?*

I knew what?

Something wasn't right. Something ISN'T right.

Nick sighs impatiently.

—here at ViaLab, we want you to know, you're family.

The screen goes dark.

—

NICK and I only have a moment to exchange a short glance before Todd and Ken appear on the screen.

And that's fucking fantastic, isn't it? Todd says. *Everyone gets paid, and no one talks. Well I'm a product of this company, don't I get a say? Those men, those "scientists" did things to us that are unforgivable. Unspeakable. How could these people not wonder why a few cells and some blood in a vial was worth so much? Is it really so easy to turn a blind eye when money is involved?*

Ken says, *since we don't exist, we have no rights. Since we're not born to a mother and a father, we belong to a company. We're no different than a new printer or an office chair. We're accessories.*

We're property, Todd says.

And since the government makes so much money from ViaLab and private investors, they look the other way, Ken says.

They did these experiments, Todd says, tears in his eyes.

They ran tests. Simulations. Made us think we were the real us. Made us remember we're just clones. Copies.

Ken says, *at times, it seemed like we didn't even exist. We didn't belong in this world. And because of the mind-link, it was damn near impossible to feel anything while the others lived. So, Mr. Z helped us put this all in motion. We needed release. And we wanted revenge.*

Todd continues, *By the time we all escaped ViaLab the first time, the scientists involved with the cloning process—and behind all of the agonizing tests and torture—were all gone. But we still wanted them dead. Mr. Z said he had the perfect way to take care of them without putting us in harm's way. We had to trick people into believing that they were doing the right thing. Paying them handsomely, of course. The ViaLab way.*

We weren't worried about these guys seeing us, Ken says, *they hadn't seen us since we were still children. But Mr. Z still hoped for a flicker of recognition. He wanted a way for these sick fucks to know who had come knocking, and he found it. He got lucky, really. Seeing how feisty his original was.*

That's right, Todd says. *Mr. Z was a natural leader, having been the last test subject ViaLab ever produced using cloning, he had all the "bells and whistles," and he had an incredibly strong power of persuasion over his original. The mind-link so strong that personality traits of one would blend to the other constantly, though they had never met. Mr. Z could control him, even during his sleep. It was like having his own avatar in some fucked-up video game.*

The thing is, Ken says, *most originals don't even know they have clones out there. When our parents made the money they made from our "experiments," they told their friends about it. They knew a family in dire need of a financial miracle.*

And lady luck was on their side, Todd says. *There was one slot open.*

24

THE MAN IN FRONT OF THE CURTAIN

NICK RAISES HIS SHOTGUN AND DESTROYS EVERY MONITOR IN the room. Blast after blast sends buckshot pellets ricocheting off the walls. Glass flies in all directions as fuses pop and smoke fills the room.

But the intercom system is still playing the audio from the message. Problem is, over Nick's ridiculous tantrum, I can't hear a damn thing.

"You're not helping anything!" I yell. "We need to get out of here and go find them!"

After Nick unloads the last few shots in the Remington into the speakers in the ceiling, he turns to me slowly, nods, and turns toward the only door in the room. As we step back into the main room, I can still hear the voices of Todd and Ken warping through the speakers, the aural equivalent of a distorted face dripping from a wax-figure in a furnace. That is to say it is utterly indistinguishable.

"What was that about?" I ask. "All the shooting?"

"I couldn't listen to them a moment longer," Nick says. "Everything is bullshit. Lies and more bullshit from those two."

"At least they were going to tell us who Mr. Z is," I say.

"I have a feeling we'll find out soon enough," Nick says. He throws his gun over his shoulder and begins walking towards the large door on the other end of the room.

"They've got to be somewhere on the other side of that door," he says. He pulls out a couple of grenades from his pouch. "And our south-of-the-border friend isn't the only one with an affinity for big bangs."

Oh my god, Nick, I can only take so much before my panties just fall off in a sopping splash. Seriously though, he's so lame sometimes it's *almost* cool.

We put ourselves a safe distance away from the door, Nick counts to three, pulls the pin, and throws the first grenade.

Flash.

Give me fire.

Flash.

Give me fury.

Flash.

Give me a break.

Three military-grade explosives later, and we've made it through one goddamn door. And I know, this is a serious part of the story here, but I'm just so tired at this point. So ready for it to be over. And Todd and Ken's speech about ViaLab and Mr. Z only confused me further. We learned that ViaLab made clones, a lot of them. And we learned that Mr. Z is one of them. It's almost easy to feel sorry for the guy. But he manipulated Nick and I into ruining our lives. Somehow, they tricked Nick into killing the real Todd.

I know, I know. Nick murdered someone, trick or no trick. It's kind of how I got into these shenanigans to begin with.

Once the smoke has settled, Nick and I come out from

behind the pillar we used for cover and walk towards the crater in the wall.

"How's that for a key card?" Nick says. "I've got the highest-level security clearance there is!"

Rolling my eyes, I follow Nick through the smoking doorway.

"I honestly can't believe we've made it this far," I say.

"Do you think we're going to die?" Nick says. He has a smile on his face. Going out like this would be right up his alley.

"Probably," I say. There isn't a trace of joking in my voice.

"Was this worth it?" He says.

"It will be," I say.

Still walking, Nick says, "When?"

"When they're all dead," I say, simply.

"But does that make us any better than them?" Nick asks.

"We didn't start this," I say.

Or did we?

We reach the end of the hallway. Nick looks up at a camera above a large door. A red laser projects down onto his face, scanning his retinas. The door opens.

"I'm sorry to say," he says as the door opens. "But you won't be finishing it, either."

Sitting at a table in the center of the room are Todd and Ken.

"About time you got here," Ken says.

"Candy," Nick says. "You may want to take a seat."

"That's right," Todd says. "Mr. Z has a lot to explain to you."

25

SUGAR-COATING

"Wait," I say, my legs shaking as my knees threaten to collapse on themselves like the twin towers. "I don't. . ."

Nick flashes his trademark shit-eating-grin. "It's really important," he says, "that you don't freak out. Okay? Just stay with me here."

"Nick," is all I can say. The word comes out in a choked cry. "What the hell, Nick? How could you—" I say. "How could you do this? Why? It's not possible! We called him," I say. "You talked to him! You're not him!"

I realize then that neither Todd nor Ken are armed. What was stopping me from shooting both of them right now?

"Boss," Todd says, standing up.

"Sit the fuck down," Mr. Z says. "I can't believe you two. I leave for—what—two days? And you two dipshits kill the girl? I told you—"

"You told us to put her in a room," Ken says. "Sir."

"Did I ask you anything?" Mr. Z says.

"No," Ken says. "But you didn't specify—"

"You knew what you were doing!" Mr. Z screams.

"What does it matter?" Ken says. "Everyone else is dead! You said there would be no witnesses. The problem took care of itself!"

"What are they talking about Nick?" I ask.

"Are you still not getting it, you dumb bitch?" Todd says. "Is your mind too preoccupied to comprehend what's happening? Oh, I know," he says, "You're wondering if you fucked the real Todd, or the clone one. That would probably mess with me too." He winks at me.

Mr. Z raises his pistol and fires a bullet through Todd's skull. Todd's body hits the ground with a *thump* as brain and bone matter slide down the wall behind the place he stood.

"Whoa!" Ken yells. "What the fuck?"

"Go get him," Mr. Z says. "Or you're next."

Ken shuffles to the other side of the room, his eyes never leaving the gun. "You didn't have to kill him, man," he says. "That's not right! After all he's done—"

Mr. Z shoots the wall next to Ken's head. "One more word," he says. "And I won't miss."

Ken opens a small door and wheels out a gurney with a body laid out on top of it. It's Nick. He's wearing the same outfit as the man in front of me.

"You killed him," I say. "You son of a bitch!"

Ken wheels Nick over in front of me.

"Thanks," Mr. Z says, and he shoots Ken in the face. Ken's expression stays the same when he's lying on the ground.

Why?

"Touch him," Mr. Z says.

"What?" I stammer.

"Nick," he says. "Touch him. You'll find that he's sleeping. He's fine. Maybe a bit drugged, but otherwise okay."

"How long has he been here?" I demand. "Has it been you with me the whole time?"

Mr. Z barks a laugh.

"Of course not," he says. "You said it yourself. You talked to me on the phone while you two were together. Look, Candy, I need you to understand, I just wanted what he had. I wanted to spend a little time with you. I wanted to live the life I never got."

"How long?" I say. "How long has he been. . . you?"

"Not long," Mr. Z says. "Only since my guys knocked you out in the bar. Nick has been here ever since."

"Why would you kill all of your own people?" I say.

"ViaLab needed to go in a new direction," he says. "I figured if I wanted it done right, I needed to do it myself. I couldn't have you and Nick coming in here and getting killed. I have to admit, though, I wasn't expecting The Mexican to man-up like that. It was almost sad to see him go."

"You're sick," I say. "You used me for what? Some kind of game?"

"No, Candy," he says. "I told you. I wanted to feel what he felt. And I could be better for you than he ever was."

That kiss.

He continues, "I want you to run the new ViaLab with me. You've proven yourself worthy. I can make you happy, Candy. We can accomplish great things together, really. Plus," he says, "I like you for who you are. I don't care about your past." He points at Nick's body on the table. "Do you think he would feel the same if he knew about Todd?"

"Are you serious?" I ask. "Did you seriously think that you could get me here, to the end of this little game of yours, and I'd just suddenly forget all the things you've done? Was that your plan? And I'm just supposed to go run the world with you? Is that it?"

"It kind of had to happen this way," he says. "You'll

understand if you think about it. Now that the lab is destroyed, the insurance policy will pay out big time. And all of the old ViaLab employees are out of the way. No more Todds and Kens to fuck up left and right. If I played you to get this result, I'm sorry. But I want you to know that I really didn't want them to kill Christina."

"And why is that?" I ask.

"Because you cared about her," he says

—

My chest hurts, everything hurts.

"You know you'll never avoid jail if you don't come with me," he says softly. He looks at Nick's body on the table. "You have to choose," he says. "But if you choose me, you'll never see the inside of a cell."

I came here to do something.

"You know," I say. "Nick isn't perfect, but he's nowhere near as crazy as you. And I know I'll probably go to jail for the rest of my life for what you've put me though. But I just want you to know that I'd spend six lifetimes in jail before I'd spend one day with you."

I point the gun at his head and pull the trigger.

—

And that, ladies and gentlemen of the jury, is what

happened. The whole truth, nothing but the truth, and all that shit.

I'm praying you people will take into account everything you've heard in this recording and make your judgements accordingly. Just try to put yourself in my shoes. What would you have done?

After I shot Mr. Z, Nick woke up, and we were met by the police. I haven't had any contact with Nick, and I'm dying to know if he's okay. I realize that I haven't really helped him out any by telling this story, but remember this: Mr. Z was controlling Nick, making him do the things he did. Nick is a fuck-up, but he's not a bad guy. I just hope my story helps people understand his side of things too.

My trial is in a couple of days. I hope you'll have mercy on me.

My name is Candy Tran. I'm recording this because the story has to be told and because my life depends on it.

Thank you.

This ends the recorded message.

EPILOGUE

STOMACHACHE

IN A COURTROOM IN NEVADA, A MAN PRESSES **STOP** ON A small tape recorder. The air in the room is stale, the stuffiness making the old Judge feel like he could be sick at any moment.

Glancing at his watch, he sees that he has finished in just enough time to meet his old friend. If you could call him that. It seemed more to the Judge like he was being used more than anything. But the money sure was nice. And he had *four* goddamned college tuitions to pay for. God knows pounding a gavel doesn't put *that* much bread on the table.

The Judge pulls the last tape out of the player and places it in its slot in a leather briefcase. Wiping his forehead, he sees that he is sweating profusely. His chest hitches in a spasm of pain.

"Fuck!" he says to the empty courtroom. Was he *that* bothered about the girl?

The feeling passes, and The Judge chalks it up to indigestion, blaming it on his spicy Mexican lunch.

The Judge picks up the briefcase and walks out of the courtroom. In the car, he wonders why the location had changed. He had always met his old friend at the same place, a popular bar in Vegas. Suddenly they were going to meet in the middle of the desert. Given the situation, it did kind of make sense, though. Even now he is looking over his shoulder a little more than usual. Checking the rearview mirrors compulsively like a man with a tick. Or brain damage.

But after this time, he will never have to work again. Sure, he would, for a while, just to keep up appearances. But when he got good and ready, he could fucking *disappear* and live off the money forever, sipping champagne out of some Brazilian stripper's ass crack on a private beach for the rest of his days. When the reward outweighs the risk, you take the risk.

The Judge belches. His eyes start to water and he pulls off the side of the road, gathering his composure. Glancing at his GPS, he sees that he isn't far from the coordinates he was sent. He pulls the car back onto the road, sweating so much now that it's hard to hold the steering wheel.

Finally, he arrives at his destination. The Judge isn't surprised when he sees a car already parked there. Tinted windows. Tempered glass. The usual. The Judge parks his car and sits staring at the dark windshield of the vehicle opposite him. He counts to three and opens the door. The driver door of the other vehicle opens. A figure steps out.

The Judge nods in the other person's direction.

"Did you bring them?" The man asks.

"You know I did."

"Where are they?"

"In my car. But we need to talk about this."

"You didn't listen to them, did you?"

"Hell no," The Judge says. "What kind of person do you

think I am? Hey, the less I know, the better. Do you understand? In my position—"

The man laughs, interrupting the old Judge. "Why are you lying?"

"Why are you questioning me? I've done everything you've asked of me."

"Everything?"

"Everything," The Judge says.

"Well, I'll just have to take your word for it."

The Judge sighs an internal sigh of relief, his insides roiling.

"You know," The Judge says, feeling bold, "I helped you take over that damn place. All the red tape, all the shit we swept under the rug. I helped you rise to the top of that company. Why did you destroy it?"

"An experiment."

"Is everything a fucking experiment to you?"

"I can't answer that."

"Why not?" The Judge asks.

"Because it will interfere with my current experiment."

The Judge laughs, long wheezy bursts. His chest hurts again.

"Before I tell you about my current experiment," the man says, "I need to make sure everything is taken care of."

"Of course," The Judge says. He turns and pulls the briefcase out of the backseat of the car.

The man takes it from him, opens it and peeks inside. He counts the tapes.

"Do you think the girl deserves what's coming to her?" He asks.

The Judge wrinkles his face is confusion. "I . . ." he says, "I don't know. I don't know anything about her. Just that you couldn't have her talking about ViaLab. Causing trouble, the usual."

"It's like these tapes," the man says. "If you listened to them, then you'd know why Candy has to die. I admit I'm not a fan of it, but it's what she chose."

"I understand."

"How will she go?" the man says.

"Stabbing in the shower, most likely," The Judge says. "We could even make it a racial thing. God knows with a case like this, it'll get questioned no matter what we do."

"I'm not worried about that."

The Judge sighs. He says, "Is the girl going to die thinking she killed you, Z?"

"There it is," Mr. Z says.

"There what is?" The Judge says, his voice bouncing around in his own head.

"The end phase of my current experiment."

"What's your current experiment?" The Judge asks. He turns and dry-heaves. "I'm sorry," he says.

"I'm testing out this neural chemical," Mr. Z says. "A person can inhale this stuff and their body just shuts down in a matter of hours. It starts out feeling like heartburn. Amnesia sets in. Eventually you can't even move. You get trapped in your mind, writhing in internal agony, frozen like a statue until you starve to death. But you feel every bit of it. It's really gruesome stuff."

The Judge holds onto the hood of his car, gripping his chest. He falls to the ground and lies staring at Mr. Z. Tries to open his mouth, but no words come out.

"Of course," Mr. Z continues, "I needed to know if I could really trust you, so I had someone put some of the nearly-invisible powder on the underside of the last tape in the briefcase. You had to know you weren't my only contact. I've got people everywhere."

The Judge stares forward in silent horror. His skin going pale, the blue veins showing underneath.

"And since I know you've heard Candy's story," Mr. Z says, "I'll explain something to you. No, I didn't tell Candy that she shot and killed her own boyfriend. What kind of person do you think I am? We'll let her go out believing she's a hero. As for you, thank you for the tapes. I wish it didn't have to be this way, but you broke my trust, Judge."

Mr. Z walks over to where The Judge lies on the desert sand, staring at the sky. The only sign of internal torment is the fire in The Judge's eyes. Picking up both feet, Mr. Z drags The Judge over to a large pit.

"Goodbye," Mr. Z says. With his foot, he shoves The Judge into the pit along with so many others.

Mr. Z looks down at the briefcase with CANDY scrawled on the label and frowns. "You're coming with me, girl," he says. He climbs into his car, pulls out a tape labeled: One – Hindsight, and places it in the tape deck.

As he shifts the car into gear, several seconds of static play through the speakers. Then a familiar voice says, "My name is Candy Tran."

The End

August 2017 – January 2018

FROM THE AUTHOR

For those who don't already know, *Candy* is my most ambitious experiment to date. I had just received word from Bloodshot Books that *Tamer Animals* wouldn't release until nearly a year after its acceptance, which is pretty normal for the publishing world, but I had been hyping the book up for a while, and I wanted to give my dedicated fans something to keep their interest until then. So, I asked the members of Justin M. Woodward Fan Club on Facebook if they would be interested in a weekly serial story which would be on Wattpad, and totally free. There was interest, and *Candy* was born. Candy is heavily inspired by the works of one of my favorite authors, (especially in my teens) Chuck Palahniuk, as well as films like Seven Psychopaths and Pulp Fiction. There's just something about this way of storytelling that appeals to me.

Not long after starting the story we welcomed our second son, Lucas, into the world, and not long after that, I changed jobs and writing became infinitely harder to accomplish. But because of my goal I set for myself, *Candy* was still released every Saturday (with the exception of Christmas, where I truly found myself unable to work). And trust me when I say that I was still writing the chapter many weeks, just hours or even minutes before it was released. And most of the time I had no idea where the story was going. I just let Candy and Nick take me where they were going.

I really hope you guys enjoyed this one. It was a lot of fun to write and I think I captured the style I was going for perfectly. Please don't forget to review this one on Amazon and Goodreads! And please pick up another book of mine if you've enjoyed this one.

Oh, and if you're worried about Candy, don't be. She's a resourceful girl.

See you next time.

- Justin.

ABOUT THE AUTHOR

Justin M. Woodward is an author from Headland, Alabama. He lives with his wife and two small boys.

He has been writing since 2015, with *Candy* being his third full-length novel.

You can keep up with him on social media, and on www.justinmwoodward.com

You can follow him on the following social media accounts.

Twitter: twitter.com/justinmwoodward

Instagram: instagram.com/justinmwoodward

Facebook: facebook.com/JustinMWoodwardFiction

Copyright © 2018 by Justin M. Woodward,
simple bicycle publishing
ISBN-13: 978-0997940916
ISBN-10: 0997940913

Edited by: Alison R. Woodward
Cover art by: Chaz Garner
www.justinmwoodward.com